Ground
Rules

A Salt Mine Novel

Joseph Browning   Suzi Yee

Text Copyright © 2019 by Joseph Browning and Suzi Yee

Published by Expeditious Retreat Press
Cover by J Caleb Design
Edited by Elizabeth VanZwolle

For information regarding Joseph Browning and Suzi Yee's novels and to subscribe to their mailing list, see their website at https://www.joseph-browning.com

To follow them on Twitter: https://twitter.com/Joseph_Browning

To follow Joseph on Facebook: https://www.facebook.com/joseph.browning.52

To follow Suzi on Facebook: https://www.facebook.com/SuziYeeAuthor/

To follow them on MeWee: https://mewe.com/i/josephbrowning

By Joseph Browning and Suzi Yee

THE SALT MINE NOVELS
Money Hungry
Feeding Frenzy
Ground Rules
Mirror Mirror
Bottom Line
Whip Smart
Rest Assured

Chapter One

Great Missenden Abbey, Buckinghamshire, UK
21st of June, 9:00 p.m. (GMT+1)

"How did I get booked for this, Alistair?" the beautiful blonde woman in the backseat complained into her phone. She was in her mid-twenties, and the driver felt like he knew her from the telly, but couldn't place her.

"Gemma doll, *A Bump in the Night* is a big hit in the States." The phone was loud enough that the driver could hear the oozing reply. "If you ever want to get out of the East End and onto the silver screen, you've got to get your face out there. This is one of the things you really need to do. It's a gateway into the American market."

"But it goes on until sunrise! I'm going to look terrible at six in the morning without any sleep."

"Don't exaggerate, Gemma. You know it only goes on until three, and then you've got a private room in the abbey until noon tomorrow."

"But it doesn't end at three, Alistair; they're still going to be filming me when I'm sleeping!" she objected petulantly.

"That's part of the appeal of the show, baby—voyeurism. There's going to be thousands of guys watching you writhe

3

about in your nightie who'll be wishing they were in bed with you. Give 'em a bit of a show and get the buzz out."

Gemma definitely knew how to be watched, and that thought mollified the actress to an extent. Her next question lacked the insolent overtones of her previous statements, "But what if something actually happens?"

"What?! You think something paranormal's actually going to happen?" the voice across the line responded with a laugh. "There's no such thing as ghosts, Gemma. The show's just scripted television for the brainless masses in the US, and those are the exact same brainless masses you want to attract when the next *Rapid and Raging* movie's looking for local cast in London."

"But my mum's seen a ghost before, and she's terrified that I'm going to be on it." The driver could tell it just wasn't her mum that was afraid.

"The show's just a big fake, GG," the voice said, using her nickname. "But hey, I can hear that you're worried. I get that; I'm hearing you," he offered the veneer of affirmation. "Just remember—nothing's going to happen. Don't let your brain fake you out. Don't jump at shadows in the corner of the room just because you're worked up."

The young actress chose not to respond, staring out the window of the car into the gloaming of the English countryside, unconvinced by her agent's words but equally certain that her objections would not be taken seriously, either. Alistair waited for her to reply, but after a long moment of silence, he became concerned—Gemma always had something to say, even if it wasn't particularly insightful or germane. He was starting to appreciate just how deep this went for her.

He softened his tone and changed his pitch, "Gemma, if you start feeling scared, just play into it. Act it up. Sell your fear and make the audience feel it right with you. This is your chance to get your foot in the door on American telly, doll, and that's where the real money is. Isn't that what we both want?"

Whatever her response, the driver heard nothing more as the wheels of his car ground into the gravel drive leading to Great Missenden Abbey. Two large transits featuring the *A Bump in the Night* logo were parked in the lot, along with about a dozen other vehicles. "We're here, miss," the driver announced, pulling to a stop before the massive gothic revival main house.

As the name suggested, Great Missenden Abbey was founded by William de Missenden for the Arrouaisian Order of Augustinians in 1133. After centuries of religious use, it fell into heresy and disrepair, and was eventually disbanded in 1538—the same year the abbey church was torn down. It lay empty for decades before a country house was built incorporating many parts of the still-standing structure. That house stood until the 1980s when a fire gutted it, and much of the current edifice had to be rebuilt from the ground up. Now, the grand home mostly served as a scenic wedding location and a bed and breakfast.

Gemma didn't know any of its history—history was boring—but she knew of the legends. The notorious Black Monk of Missenden could be seen wandering the village and the abbey, as could two noble brothers who had been buried on horseback. And that was in addition to the "regular" ghosts found in every small village in the UK: scorned lovers, despondent servants, and wealthy madmen who refused to quietly shuffle off the mortal coil. There was a reason why *A Bump in the Night* had chosen Missenden Abbey as their first international ghost hunting location.

The young actress stepped out into the sultry air. Record high temperatures were afflicting the nation, and although the sun was nearly down, its warmth still dominated the land. The driver popped the boot so she could retrieve her small day luggage—*so much for his tip!*—and she had to pull down her short khaki Helmut Lang skirt that had ridden up as she bent down. She roughly closed the boot, letting her displeasure be known, and angrily swayed into the welcomed air conditioning as she entered the bustling foyer.

"Gemma!" a fleshy man in a black t-shirt called out as the doors closed behind her. He was nearly six feet tall, with a thick, ungroomed beard. Gemma estimated he was at least eighteen stone, and she was proud of herself for keeping her smile perfect during his clammy handshake.

"It's great to have you here," he gushed in some strange

American accent. "Let me acquaint you with the crew and get you into your room." As he introduced her to the group, a bunch of late-twenties-early-thirties Americans, she quickly assessed that they had no experience interacting with someone as alluring as she was. In the thirty minutes it took to get everything set up, she'd already caught more than half of them stealing glances at her curves when they thought she couldn't see. As she unpacked, she resolved to use that to her advantage. The more the cameras were on her, the better.

Shooting began half an hour after sunset, the crew splitting into two groups of three to cover more ground. Gemma's group included the two founders of the show. They began in the foyer and moved throughout the public areas of the abbey, holding something called an EMF reader that was supposed to detect ghosts. As they went, they asked questions, such as "Is there anyone here who would like to speak with us?" and "If there's something you'd like to say, please let us know." As they went, two cameramen circled around them, catching the group from different angles.

It wasn't shot like a traditional show, where the actors had set blocking in relation to the cameras, but Gemma paid close attention to the cameramen and quickly picked up their movements. She knew they had to have a pattern to catch different point of views while keeping the main actors in view but not each other. After an hour of filming, she found a way to ensure she was in every shot. She was particularly proud when she orchestrated a scene she was certain would air—she "accidentally" dropped the EMF reader while both cameras were rolling from behind, and she bent down in her short Helmut Lang to retrieve it. That shot would not end up on the proverbial cutting room floor.

After dropping the reader on a thick carpet—she didn't want to pay for any damages—her group moved to the exterior while the other group came inside. Two hours had passed, and nothing unusual had happened.

"It is always this quiet?" she asked Dave, the fleshy one, while both groups took toilet breaks.

"Sometimes," he responded and quickly rushed on, trying to make what he did sound interesting, "but other times it gets real freaky, and you have to fight to stop yourself from running away. Bob and I are expecting more from the exterior than the interior here. We're going to spend an hour or so where the old church used to be. The abbey's graveyard was back there, and all the tombstones were hauled away and used to build one of the inns in town, so we're expecting there will be some activity there. After all, no one wants to be forgotten."

Gemma felt the first inklings of fear, and it came across in her wan smile.

"But you don't have to worry about it," Dave reassured her. "We've never been hurt or anything on our investigations. Mostly we just hear strange things, and sometimes see something odd. You're perfectly safe."

His assurances had the opposite effect, but there wasn't anything she could do about it now. They trundled out into a field near the abbey and waited for an hour in near darkness under thick clouds. Eventually boredom set in and—feeling a bit peeved with Alistair for making her do this stupid show—she decided to take the spotlight and make the best of it. She suddenly jumped and squealed, "Something touched me! Something's touched me!"

"Where?" Bob demanded, bringing his thermal camera to bear.

"On my left shoulder!" she replied, trying to nail the perfect amount of mid-level fear; she needed to keep the upper registers open if she wanted to step up the tension later on. All the cameramen focused on her as she turned her shoulder toward Bob. She made sure her chin was up so that they caught the full height of her magnificent cheekbones.

"Nothing's showing on thermal," he declared, looking down at the tiny screen. "We might be able to see more during analysis."

"It felt really cold, like being touched by an ice lolly," Gemma lied as she rubbed her shoulder. She figured that was the right thing to say, given Dave and Bob's constant statements about "cold spots."

"Awesome!" Dave exclaimed. "Not very many people get to experience a physical encounter. Consider yourself lucky." She only smiled in response, making sure at least one of the cameras caught her full on.

The rest of the night was equally as tiresome. A lot of sitting, intermixed with walking around asking questions in empty fields or rooms. They finally packed it in around three, the entire crew thanking Gemma for being there before she trundled off to bed. While she'd unpacked after she arrived, she'd carefully noted where her room's cameras were located and she made sure to undress and change just out of their range, except for a few well-placed "accidents" that could make it past American censors. *They were such prudes!* She tucked herself into bed and went straight to sleep, happy that she hadn't had any real supernatural experiences. She wouldn't tell Alistair that, though—best not to tell him he's right too often.

Once the cameras were off and their incredibly hot guest host was away, the guys could talk amongst themselves about how sexy she was. And that accent! They didn't have classy women like that in Connecticut. But eventually their fatigue returned; no matter how desirable she was, there was only so much that talking about it could animate them—they'd been up for nearly twenty-four hours. They were nearing the dangerous loopy phase, and handling thousands of dollars of equipment when tired wasn't a good idea. They packed their portables away and called it a night, retreating to their respective rooms. It took Dave less than three minutes to draw the curtains—the sun came up early in England during the summer—and get out of his clothes and into bed. It didn't take him that long to fall asleep.

Sometime later, Dave Thompson, co-creator and producer of *A Bump in the Night*, woke to the sounds of screaming coming from Gemma's room.

Chapter Two

Detroit, Michigan, USA
26th of June, 6:06 a.m. (GMT-4)

David Wilson lay half-awake in bed as the blare of the Postal Service morning fleet departed for their deliveries. The unmistakable rumble of dozens of delivery vehicles fully roused him from his semi-consciousness, as they'd done with such consistency that he'd forgone the use of an alarm since he'd moved into the 500. His private sanctum sanctorum, 500 10th Street was a converted warehouse customized with dozens of protections against various potential threats. He'd installed these defenses, because David Emrys Wilson wasn't the average briefcase-carrying, middle-aged businessman. Not only was he a magician, he was one in the service of the Salt Mine, the secret cross-organization of the CIA and the FBI tasked with protecting the USA, and the greater world at large, from supernatural threats of all kinds.

After a minute, the ruckus died down, and he opened his eyes to the tiniest sliver of the sun peaking over the horizon. It cast a rectangle of clear white light against the dark red brick of the western wall of his bedroom. Summer days in Detroit started at the perfect time for him, so he'd left his curtains open during the night. If for some reason the trucks didn't wake him, the sun would.

He rose and went through his series of morning stretches. Wilson was a small man, only five and a half feet tall, and lean. He was a little bit heavier than he was when he graduated from Camp Peary long ago, but the added pounds were muscle. He'd finally figured out his dietary requirements, and now he was a compact one hundred fifty pounds. He had a boxer's body, albeit one littered with scars from his all-too-close encounters with the supernatural.

Eventually, the call of the automated coffee pot proved greater than his need for flexibility. Breakfast was a simple affair: fried eggs and toast followed by a veggie-and-protein shake. He was a man of efficient routine, and had honed breakfast—from start to finish—to less than six minutes. Within the half hour, he was dressed for work—coffee cup in one hand, Korchmar Monroe attaché in the other—and down the ornately adorned wrought iron spiral staircase leading from his fourth-story apartment to the ground floor of the warehouse. More than just decoration, the silver runes and sigils etched into the staircase ensured it remained off limits to supernatural forces, other than those he wished—just another precaution in his line of work.

All the ground and first-floor windows of the 500 were bricked up, and an inverted, reinforced-concrete talus wall lined the interior of the warehouse. It was ten feet thick at the base and narrowed to a single foot twenty feet above the ground—strong enough to resist anything less than proper artillery or a shaped detonation charge. The only entrance into the 500 was blocked by a massive six-ton steel garage door that had teeth on its bottom, ensuring it locked into the ground like a jaw.

Wilson's metallic British racing green 911 was parked where the spiral staircase debouched. He had to get the color custom, but he thought the expense worth it—one classic deserved another. He waited to raise the garage door until his attaché was in the passenger's seat, the engine was started, and all the doors were locked. He was a careful man by nature, made more so by experience.

It was a quick drive to the Salt Mine when the weather was clear. It was located on Zug Island, whose only other occupant was Detroit Iron Works, an iron foundry in operation since 1901. The Salt Mine's cover was Discretion Minerals, an actual salt mining company founded in 1911 and purchased by the CIA for the MKULTRA project in 1955. Wilson's primary alias was Davis Watson, Director of Acquisitions for Discretion Minerals, a vague enough title that provided cover for any international movements. After all, there were minerals and small mining companies everywhere, and businesses were always interested in acquiring both.

He exchanged the usual vapid pleasantries with the gate guard—there were only two bridges onto the island, and one was exclusively for large truck deliveries. Wilson backed into a parking space in front of the elevators leading down into the mine. He set his alarm and, after making sure he could enter alone, entered the elevator. With a flick of a titanium key into the slot, it descended to a secret floor, the first floor of the Salt Mine.

"Good Morning, Wilson," the ever-chipper voice of Angela Abrams crackled out through an old and tinny speaker.

"And to you," Wilson returned the greeting, his voice echoing slightly in the all-metal room. Abrams sat opposite the elevator, behind enough ballistic glass to stop a grenade. "Be a doll and buzz me in," he requested with raised eyebrows.

"You know I can't do that," she responded with a soft smile, still enjoying their little game, even though she was now happily dating. "Put your belongings in the slot," she said, opening a hole in the left wall where he placed his Korchmar Monroe and Glock 26. The machine behind the wall whirred away, subjecting his belongings to various examinations and ensuring that nothing unwanted entered the Mine.

"Harry and I had dinner at El Barzon last night. They have the best mole I've ever had! You should try it some time," she suggested as they waited. She was always suggesting things for him to do.

"I'll have to look into it," he replied, even though he had no intention of doing so. He wasn't a foodie. Food was fuel, nothing more.

The machine beeped its happy-okay noise, and Abrams buzzed him in through the thick metal door. He picked up his case and his firearm on the other side and walked down a long metal corridor that ended in two elevators. He opened the left doors via a palm sensor, but the elevator wouldn't move without activating the internal palm and retinal scanners. Wilson had access down to the fifth floor, where his office was located; only the sixth floor was off limits to him.

Buried 426 feet below the surface, the sixth floor was the orderly domain of Chloe and Dot, conjoined twins with eidetic memories, who acted as librarians for the vast tomes housed in the saline tombs. As such, the twins were experts on all things supernatural and ideal instructors for the Mine's agents. Under their tutelage, agents became mindful practitioners of the arts to augment the skills honed through FBI and CIA training.

The sixth floor was more than just a destination for magical learning, however; it was also the gateway deeper into the earth, accessible only by another elevator found within the library. There were twelve more floors burrowed into the ancient salt deposit—storage for the magical items the Mine had accumulated over the decades, as well as holding cells. The lowest level, about 850 feet away from the sun, held but one room and one occupant: Furfur, a Great Earl of Hell. Wilson did not like speaking with the devil, but he did so when needs must.

Wilson held his hand and eye to their respective scanners;

once his identity was authenticated, he pressed the fifth-floor button. The air in the elevator was desiccated, like all the air in the compound; moisture didn't hang around when surrounded by salt on all sides. The doors opened to a large communal room populated by leather furniture with a sleek, Scandinavian design. Decorated in black and white that accented the natural layers of black and white in the salt walls, the furniture could comfortably hold dozens, although only six fellow agents worked on this floor with Wilson.

He quickly ascended the carved salt ramp and strode down a corridor flanked by thick wooden doors embossed with brass nameplates to his office, the last on the left. As he passed, he subconsciously read the names on the doors. He'd known thirteen of them personally in his years in the Mine. None of them had retired.

Another palm scan triggered the heavy clunk of his door's lock, and the door swung back to reveal his office, decorated with Art Deco furniture he'd moved down himself with the helpful bribe of a twenty-five-year-old Laphroaig—one of the younger agents had a yen for peaty scotch.

There were two folders waiting for him on his desk. The first was the worn manila folder marked OFFICIAL – SM EYES ONLY that always contained the daily intel update culled from their larger CIA and FBI briefings. The green one labeled AGENT RESTRICTED – SM EYES ONLY in bright red ink meant something important was happening. He placed his attaché next to the table and immediately opened the more intriguing of the two folders. It contained information on Damon Warwick, Comptroller and Auditor General of the Institute of Tradition, Wilson's cover for the mission Leader would assign him later today.

*****

"Leader will see you now, Fulcrum," David LaSalle's precise tenor voice informed Wilson. LaSalle was a towering private secretary-slash-bodyguard for the head of the Salt Mine, who was nothing like her assistant. Leader was petite, a good half-foot shorter than Wilson, and inevitably dressed in jeans and some type of self-fabricated top. She knitted, sewed, and crocheted; Wilson wouldn't be surprised if he found out she even spun her own yarn. Her hair was gray, peppered with black, and she had an incredible will.

Recruited out of the CIA, Wilson was an accomplished magician and spy, a formidably dangerous and powerful man made even more so because he didn't look it. However, Leader was something different. She conveyed a near-physical sense of inevitable determination. It had taken him years to finally relax enough in her presence to breathe without thinking about it. He did not know her real name or anything about her background, and he had the feeling it was best that way. She never called him anything but Fulcrum; to her, he was an instrument of leverage, to be used when a subtle push could change affairs or—when all else failed—as a weapon launched against their enemies.

"Take a seat, Fulcrum," she said tersely. "Last Friday, a British television actress, Gemma Green, was attacked in one of the rooms of Great Missenden Abbey, Buckinghamshire. She had just finished filming as a guest host for the ghost-hunting show *A Bump in the Night*."

"Deceased?"

"No, but injured. She's claiming, as are the creators of the show, that she was attacked by a ghost."

Wilson knew he wouldn't be sitting there if Leader didn't think the claim was credible, or at least plausible. "I thought we had an arrangement with the ghosts of Great Missenden? Don't we have a placater in place?"

"We do on both accounts." Leader looked down at the file on her desk. "Mrs. Vivienne Clark, age seventy-one; organizes ghost tours at Great Missenden and nearby areas."

"She's getting up in years," Wilson spoke euphemistically, uncertain of just how close Leader was to becoming a septuagenarian.

"Indeed," she agreed neutrally. "You'll need to establish if she's been doing what we pay her to do, and if not, why. More worrisome is that the *A Bump in the Night* creators are promising to release their footage early—Friday after next." Leader didn't need to state the necessity of obfuscating legitimate spirit activity from the general public.

"Where are they located?" Wilson was only passingly familiar with the show. It wasn't the sort of thing he would watch for entertainment, and the data analysts in the Mine watched every episode, so there was no need for him to pay attention to it.

"Danbury, Connecticut," Leader answered. Wilson's face showed no recognition, so she continued, "It's a small town in the western part of the state; close to the New York border. Your primary task is to prevent that footage from being made available to the public."

"And then find out what's going on in the UK?" Wilson wagered a guess.

"Precisely," she responded, sliding over a file. "Within you'll find information on the show and the injured actress, as well as our arrangement with the ghosts at Great Missenden and Vivienne Clark."

Wilson did a quick flip-through. "How's the press been?"

"Typical. They ran with the story, but it's not gaining any more traction than you'd think, except in the expected rags. There's a strong undercurrent that it's all just a publicity stunt among the more-serious outlets."

"Seems rather over-the-top for just a stunt," Wilson responded dryly as he closed the file and secured it under his arm.

Leader shrugged. "It's easier than believing she was really

attacked. Regardless, it works in our favor."

"When do I fly out?"

"You're booked on the 6:15 to Hartford. That should give you time to get your affairs in order, meet with Harold, and make it to the airport." Wilson checked his Girard-Perregaux and nodded. "We need those recordings to disappear, Fulcrum, and we need to understand what's happening in the Great Missenden ghostly community."

Chapter Three

Detroit, Michigan, USA
26th of June, 2:00 p.m. (GMT-4)

"Nice of you to drop by," Dot commented sarcastically, after being informed that Wilson wasn't on the sixth floor to visit her and Chloe.

"It's not you, it's me," he quipped as he walked away. He wasn't a joker by nature, but Dot occasionally drew it out of him. Over the years of working together, they'd found their world-views were remarkably similar and they connected on a deep nihilistic level that Chloe viscerally didn't understand, even though she and Dot had been literally joined at the hip their whole lives. Wilson caught a rare Dot-smile out of the corner of his eye before losing sight of the twins behind the massive shelves, groaning with books in all imaginable forms.

A few quick turns down a long corridor brought him to the armory, the domain of Harold Weber. Weber was well versed in firearms and weaponry, as well as current covert designs of the CIA and oppositional groups—a veritable master of tech. For example, he was the person responsible for the development of the covert lining used in the three special suitcases Wilson kept pre-packed for travel in his office, which were now standard-issue for all Salt Mine operatives.

That said, what made Weber truly exceptional was his constant tinkering with the latest mundane espionage equipment, melding them to magical purposes. Not all of his prototypes panned out, which was why his workshop was far enough away from the librarians and their stacks, but when he found the perfect fusion of mundane, covert, and supernatural, it was spectacular.

Weber was an old man—Wilson assumed he was past retirement age—but he was spry and had a facile mind. He had the air of one who'd only stop working after he was put in the ground. Of German background via Belarus, he had escaped to the west early in his life and was known to mutter to himself in German, Russian, or English depending on his mood. He was organized and fastidious without being fussy. Besides his ingenuity, what Wilson appreciated most about Weber was that he cut to the chase—the inventor didn't want to waste his time and in so doing, didn't waste anyone else's either.

"Fulcrum," he spoke as Wilson's figure darkened his door.

"Weber," Wilson replied. It was what sufficed as a greeting between the familiar colleagues. Weber was wearing his standard work apron with a multitude of pockets, and his white wispy hair was doing its best impersonation of the torch on the Statue of Liberty. Wilson did not admire his grooming, but the agent reluctantly admitted he nailed the absent-minded inventor look more than he missed.

The old man waved him past the tables filled with various objects and brought him to the back of the room. "Here's what I've prepared for this mission. You're getting an updated saltcaster with some refinements based upon Lancer's feedback regarding her usage in San Diego—the salt dispersal should have a few more feet of range and use half a gram less per blow." He picked up what looked like a vape pen and passed it over. "You'll have five uses before you need refilling. Don't forget that if you twist to the left, you can also use it as an electronic jammer with a ten-meter range."

Wilson turned the item over in his hands. "I'm assuming a right twist allows one to vape?"

Weber gave him an of-course-it-does look and continued, "Next is this little beauty, perhaps the best thing I have ever created!" He held up a piece of sanded olivine, about the size of an aglet, with tiny, miniature silver sigils ground into it. "You place it under your tongue and it allows you to communicate with the dead, even if you don't speak their language."

Wilson's normally impassive face lit up—one of the main problems with contacting the dead was language. Even if both parties technically spoke the same language, there were huge differences in grammar, vocabulary, and usage over time. Some of the spirits at Great Missenden Abbey died more than six hundred years ago, and their English was radically different than modern English—and that was not even taking Wilson's American English into account.

"It works?" His suspicious nature caught up with his enthusiasm.

Weber proudly smiled. "It really works, but the prototype only lasts for an hour or so. It dissolves as you use it—a little gritty, but otherwise harmless."

"How many do you have?" Wilson inquired, which was his way of asking how many he would have on his upcoming mission.

"I've made three, but only two are available to you. They take considerable time to make; use them judiciously, if you must." He reluctantly handed over a small velvet pouch, like a parent giving his kid the keys to the car. Wilson felt the two hard objects within as he placed it in his breast pocket.

"Lastly, we have updated knives for your suitcase. They are still a carbon fiber and metallic glass mixture, but I've managed to add in some iron, silver, and copper without losing any of their benefits. I believe they'll be effective against most supernatural creatures now. It's a small update, but one that could prove beneficial."

Wilson looked down at the two thin blades, matching the pairs in every one of his suitcases. "Are we getting new cases?"

"No. Just the knives. Again, I only have three, so I'm going to send you out with two of the prototypes. Eventually, we intend to replace and update all the cases for our agents." He handed over the new pair to Wilson. "Just leave me your old ones when you get the chance."

Wilson accepted the blades, carefully holding them in his left hand; he didn't want to prick or slice his suit. The knives were frighteningly sharp, even if they didn't hold their edge for very long.

Weber paused and ran down his mental checklist. "Ah, regarding ammunition. How are your supplies? Do you have enough left over from your last visit to the UK?"

"I should have plenty—all but a few shots."

Weber nodded, "Nasty bit of business that one, but you stand here today, *so ende gut, alles gut.*"

"*Jawolh, Herr Weber. Jawolh.*"

*****

After sitting on the tarmac for nearly half an hour, the engines roared and Wilson felt the familiar pressure against the airline seat. He was glad to finally be in the air, and relaxed as the plane leveled out the steepness of its ascent. Once again, he had a middle seat, which happened more often than he liked, but that was the consequence of booking on short notice. At least he was between two women this time—one appeared to be a college student and the other a likely business traveler, based on her appearance and accoutrements. It boded well that no one had tried to exchange small talk with him while they'd waited. Over his many years of flying, he'd found that women did not strike up conversations during flights unless they had a child or were above a certain age, and he'd never been attractive enough to garner special treatment.

Once they were solidly in the air, he settled in for the short flight and returned to his files regarding *A Bump in the Night*. The show started six years before on the cable channel Visionaries, airing Fridays at 9:00 p.m. It was a surprise hit for the small channel, allowing them to pull in nearly $20,000 per thirty-second commercial on the most-recent season. That kind of ad revenue was small fry by industry standards—roughly a quarter of what a solid show on one of the big networks could command mid-week—but it was considered a massive success for Visionaries.

The show's success quickly spawned imitators from other smaller networks, which spurred them to create an international version of their program this year that broadcast right after the original show to increase viewer buy-in and retention—if you like ghosts, we now offer them in exotic locales with foreign accents! The untimely injury of Gemma Green occurred while filming the international incarnation of the show in what was supposed to be the season finale, but was now next in line.

The show was created by two friends, Dave Thompson and Bob Willard, who'd created the Western Connecticut Paranormal Society (WCPS) several years prior to the show. They had a total of twelve "investigators" split between the two shows as well as six crewmembers for audio and visual. All of the crew lived in Danbury, Connecticut, excepting two crewmembers who lived in Hartford. Wilson carefully ran down the personal address list, ensuring that the building WCPS used as its headquarters wasn't also the private residence of one of the members. Thankfully, it wasn't.

He looked up the office address online and walked around the nearby area using street view. It was a freestanding house, originally a two-story Richardsonian Romanesque built in 1895—according to city records—but somewhere along the line, it was increased to three full stories. It was a brick structure featuring two large Syrian arches folding over the second-story balcony, and where others would only see architecture, Wilson saw opportunity. The balcony would be his way in; once there, he'd have plenty of time to make a quiet and secure entry, probably through a window, as they were less likely to have an alarm. The balcony's brick half-wall would provide all the cover he needed.

Behind the house, with a field separating them, was an ice cream parlor—the oldest in the town—which had just transitioned to its summer hours, meaning it would be open late. While this shouldn't affect any of his movements—the shop still closed well before he would typically embark on a covert infiltration—he wasn't a fan of the large open parking lot in the near proximity of his objective, as horny teenagers will find any place they can to enjoy each other's company.

Wilson left the map for a more-detailed exploration once he was in his hotel and started watching a selection of clips the Salt Mine analysts had gleaned from the most-recent four seasons of A Bump in the Night. Each of the collated scenes occurred inside the home office; he thanked the gods of necessity that made producers want to keep shooting costs as low as possible while he familiarized himself with the interior of his target. They didn't know it when they were filming, but they were making his job that much easier.

"Excuse me," the business woman on his right interrupted his reconnaissance, "but I can't help but notice you're interested in the paranormal."

Of all the people to sit next to, Wilson thought to himself. *Such is the hazard of the middle seat.* "I'm a TV show producer for CBS and we're scouting out potential acquisitions," he replied coldly, not bothering to remove his earbuds.

"Oh, how interesting!" she exclaimed, slightly turning her shoulders toward him.

Familiar with that signal, he nipped the conversation in the bud. "I'm also gay and in a committed relationship, so if you don't mind, I need to get back to work." She was offended, as was the intent, and stopped talking to him. Wilson made sure to tilt his screen toward the college student, who was oblivious to the world and totally engrossed in a tablet game that apparently involved seeing how far you could toss a luchador elephant around the screen. As one does.

He watched all of the excerpts, making a mental note of the headquarters' layout and burning the faces and body language of the WCPS members into his memory. It was unlikely he'd meet them, but if he did, knowing their names, faces, and movements would make any magics easier—the more you knew about someone, the easier the work.

Chapter Four

Danbury, Connecticut, USA
26th of June, 10:00 p.m. (GMT-4)

"Vanilla, please," Wilson said to the teenager behind the counter. "On a sugar cone."

"Just plain vanilla?" she asked dubiously, waving her hand at the counter of addable treats.

"Just vanilla," he confirmed.

She grabbed a scooper from the warm water and slid it through the tub of silky pale yellow ice cream, forming a sphere before molding it into the flat-bottomed cone. She handed it over and Wilson paid, dropping the change into the tip jar. He walked outside into the night, making room in the small shop for the next customer. It had been a hot, muggy day, and the heat was just starting to dissipate, even if the humidity wasn't.

He'd driven in from Hartford, checked into his hotel, and stopped at Earl's Ice Cream to get his first eyes-on. He sat down on one of the painted benches away from the neon lights attracting bugs and looked at the headquarters for the Western Connecticut Paranormal Society. He licked the quickly melting treat, displeased with what he saw.

The building appeared empty and closed for the night—

there were no lights on inside. That would have been good news were it not for the small flashing red lights blinking cheerfully away within the windows. It didn't necessarily mean they had a decent security system, but the fact that they came from every window suggested they were conscientious about safeguarding their headquarters. If they did employ commercial security services, it wasn't your standard homeowner operation—they typically used yard signs or window decals as a deterrent to potential thieves. Wilson reluctantly realized he might have to call off his planned infiltration until he could examine the area during the day.

Equally bothersome was one of the two cameras at Earl's. It was on a power pole and had the full parking lot in view—including the WCPS office and the empty field between it and Earl's. It effectively took the entire back and west side of the structure off the table, as the camera was too far away to disrupt with his current technological means.

He thought as he whittled away at his cone in silence, reflexively mashing the remaining ice cream deeper into the progressively shrinking stem with the flat of his tongue. If approaching the back through the empty field wasn't possible, he needed to scout out the neighboring homes in the area to see if there were any dogs that would get bent out of shape were he to walk by during the middle of the night. No time like the present, he thought as he popped the last of the cone into his mouth and dropped his napkin in the recycling.

Wilson drove around the corner to scout the front of WCPS, parking a few blocks away in front of a house with a "for sale" sign. He locked the rental and casually walked down the street, paying attention to which lights were on, which houses had oil spots on the street in front of them— suggesting there were more cars that had yet to park— and most importantly, who were dog owners and where said dogs were kept. As he strolled, the occasional bark broke the calm of the listless summer night, but all of them were interior yappy dog variety, as opposed to the large yard-dog bark that could prove troublesome.

He had made the decision to keep to the opposite side of the street of the headquarters when he pulled up, just in case they had additional security features he didn't spot from Earl's. It was a hollow victory to discover his suspicious nature justified when he passed by under the watch of two motion-following cameras—one on the front porch and one on the corner of the second-story balcony.

It was just his luck to get a bunch of tech-heads who were worried about burglars; even the trellis for the wisteria had been removed. They should have named it the Western Connecticut Paranoid Society, he groused as he passed the building across the street. Wilson hadn't packed heavy, and considered his two possible courses of action as he turned the corner away from the house: proceed with the infiltration he had originally planned to do later tonight or call in a full infiltration package.

He didn't worry much about the cameras; he could easily

disable them. The alarm system, on the other hand, was worrisome. Having every window openly alarmed niggled at him and made him worry that there would be other sensors in place, like a vibration detector. Jamming those required tech he didn't currently have. It was just a hunch, but he knew not to ignore them when they came to him.

Frustrated by the hitch, he walked back to his car; this was supposed to be an overnight hit. He had more important things to do in England, but circumstances put this at the top of his list. He made another circuit, taking a slightly different route this time to check out the adjacent streets. By the time he returned to the car, he knew he'd have to wait.

Once back at the hotel, Wilson sent in a request for additional equipment, altered his flight plans, and revisited the Salt Mine files on *A Bump in the Night* to see if he could find any easy cracks to exploit, particularly with Thompson and Willard, the two creators. One of them had to be behind the over-the-top security, and that could be their weakness.

*****

Late the following morning, Wilson got the information from the Salt Mine he was waiting for—the name of the security firm that serviced the headquarters of Western Connecticut Paranormal Society. Last night he'd noticed a decidedly anti-government tone running through the paranormal forum, particularly after they'd been audited, including a nod to the "taxes are theft!" crowd. Expecting WCPS to have aggressively deducted to reduce their tax burden, he'd requested the analysts to hunt down their tax return on the audit year and find the receipt for security expenses. From that, he had a name: Independent Alarm and Security, based out of Hartford.

In Wilson's experience, hacking a security company was often easier than hacking what they were paid to protect. He checked on the delivery time of the additional equipment he'd requested to determine if he would be able to get to Hartford and back before it arrived. Discovering it wasn't scheduled to arrive until 7:00 p.m., he made the hour drive to Connecticut's capital.

Independent Alarm and Security had an office staff of twelve and occupied a freestanding structure that had at one time been a video rental store. As Wilson entered, his face danced across several monitors, while a battery of motion, infrared, and ultrasonic detectors in the corner flashed green and red. Two women sat behind a counter—customer service, he assumed. One of them greeted him with a small nod and an upheld finger, silently asking him to wait just a moment. Her nametag said Jada.

Once she'd finished a spate of rapid typing, she looked up with a warm smile. "Thanks for your patience. What can I do for you today?"

"Davis Watson, Director of Acquisitions, Discretion

Minerals," he reported masterfully.

Jada got the distinct impression that she was supposed to know what that meant, unfortunately, she hadn't a clue. She kept up her smile despite the slight panic that was creeping in as she pulled up the schedule on the screen. She asked for clarification to buy her and the computer some time, "Pardon?"

"Davis Watson," he repeated, this time handing her one of his tastefully thick, subtle off-white business cards as he spoke. "I have a two o'clock appointment about a new account for the Deadrock Graphite mine over in Massachusetts. Sorry I'm a bit early; I wasn't sure how long it would take me to get here."

"I see," she replied knowingly. The program was taking forever to load; Jada closed down all the other windows and applications, hoping it would speed things up. "I'm sorry, the computer is running dreadfully slow today. Do you know who you have an appointment with?"

"No, my secretary set it up earlier today. I've been on the road; I just came from the mine. Pretty country up here."

She nodded and her eyes dipped to the screen—the schedule had finally loaded. Jada maintained the conversation, commenting about the scenery as she frantically worked her computer, trying to find his appointment.

"Ah, there it is! If you wouldn't mind waiting for just a second, I'll see if Mavis is ready." She pantomimed finding his appointment when Wilson knew full well that was impossible. He admired her professionalism, considering the wrench he was throwing into her orderly works. "Can I get you anything while you wait? Coffee? Water?"

"Coffee please. Two sugars, milk, and a dash of cinnamon if you have it," Wilson rattled off like it was his standard order. It was best to appear difficult and demanding right out of the gate; it would surely get back to Mavis when Jada told her she had an unexpected guest, one with a big contract opportunity once Mavis hit the web.

As anticipated, Jada left the room holding his card. Having the right props were important; despite their diminished use in business in the digital age, business cards still convinced people that things were real and important. Wilson had a card, therefore he was serious; never mind that anyone could print up a couple hundred for nearly no expense.

Jada returned a few minutes later with the desired beverage. "My apologies about the cinnamon, Mr. Watson—we don't keep any in office," she prefaced before handing it over to him. "Mavis is clearing up the last of her one o'clock and will be ready for you in just a few more minutes."

Wilson nodded his head curtly and bemusedly sipped his coffee—the only thing Mavis was clearing up was who the hell was Discretion Minerals and where was the Deadrock Graphite mine. A quick internet search would uncover plenty of information on the former, but would draw a blank on the latter, as it didn't exist.

Wilson had just finished his coffee when a middle-aged

woman came out of the back. "Mr. Watson! I'm Mavis Walker, President of Independent Alarm and Security." He shook her hand and responded with a warm "Ms. Walker." She led him to her office, mouthing pleasantries as she went.

Her mannerisms changed once they settled on opposite sides of her desk. She became laser-focused on the task at hand. "I understand Discretion Minerals is interested in using our services for security at the Deadrock Graphite mine?"

"Dreadrock Graphite, not Deadrock," Wilson falsely corrected. A subtle wave of relief rippled across Walker's face— that explained why she couldn't find out anything about the mine online. She quickly regained her game face as Wilson continued, "But yes, we've got over six hundred acres that need an entirely new protective system. We just closed the sale yesterday with Desmong, and found out that they'd let their security lapse during the purchasing period. We can't run a mine without security; the machinery and potential trespassers aside, we've explosives to safeguard. We need cameras, active guards, and most importantly, an electrical security fence with inertial sensors."

The system he was describing was a multi-million dollar solution, and Wilson could see the dollars racking up in her eyes. "What time frame are you looking….looking…" she trailed off as he finally released the will he'd been building since entering Independent Alarm and Security.

"I'm glad you've agreed to immediately cancel our contract,

Ms. Walker. The Western Connecticut Paranormal Society appreciates your professional excellence, and although we must part ways, we will speak positively about your services to any who ask," Wilson spoke as he continued pushing.

"I'm…what?" Walker's brows wrinkled for a moment. "Yes, I'm…I'm sorry to see you go, Mr.…?"

"Thompson. And you haven't made the change yet. Make the change," he ordered. She woodenly clicked away at her computer. "Make sure all our services are severed immediately, because we haven't paid our bill in three months. Once you've done that, you should send us into collections," he directed her.

"Collections," she droned.

Wilson didn't need to do that, but he was more than a little annoyed that WCPS had such a good security system that it cost him an extra day. He felt no compunction adding a little grief to their lives. He threaded more of his will—*think, think, think*—pressing hard to insure she wouldn't remember anything. "And once that's done, erase all of today's security footage for this building. You don't want it to get out into the public. Just think of the scandal!"

"Don't want any scandals," she dumbly mouthed.

"It's the only way to be sure," he reinforced his will.

Walker nodded. "The only way to be sure."

Wilson left once he was certain Walker carried out all his requests, double-checking that WCPS had lost all service—it wouldn't do for him to break in tonight just to find out that there was a twenty-four-hour cancellation delay. Mission successful, he turned on the local classical station and pointed his rental back toward Danbury.

With nothing to do until his package arrived, Wilson let the flood of endorphins wash over him, filling him with joy to the impassioned strains of Bruckner's Symphony No. 7 as he cruised down the sunny highway. While most practitioners of the arts only had to worry about karma making an appointment for a slapdown at a later date, there was a small subset whose brains lit up with its use, causing a euphoric rush. There weren't very many of them, because it was a self-regulating group—the ability to become addicted to something that is also actively trying to kill you through karma resulted in a lot of dead magic-addicted magicians.

Wilson was such a caster, and it was his discipline that kept him on the straight and narrow. He stuck to using the magic kit Weber supplied him and kept to summoning as much as possible whenever a problem required a magical solution or supernatural investigation—it was one of the few magics that didn't give Wilson a happy pill. It there had been any other way to achieve the first part of his mission without charming the President of Independent Alarm and Security, he would have done it. But there wasn't, so he enjoyed the good feedback while it lasted.

Chapter Five

Great Missenden, Buckinghamshire, UK
28th of June, 11:00 p.m. (GMT+1)

The night was clear and warm, and the small group that gathered at the Greysides opted for seats in the courtyard. Despite their recent face-to-face introduction, they had interacted online for months and the conversation flowed freely, fueled by several rounds of drinks. While they were disparate in background and age, their common interest drew them together for their first meeting in real life.

Muhammad Farah raised his glass of amber ale and proposed a toast, "To the inaugural meeting of the Chiltern Truth Seekers!" The three figures seated with him followed suit and called back, "To the Truth Seekers!" Farah, who went by Mo, was overwhelmed by a feeling of camaraderie—what could be better than getting a pint with new mates? He enjoyed the feeling, more so because he was an introverted fellow by temperament who didn't make friends easily. It didn't help that his three main interests were programming, entomology and the paranormal—it wasn't like he could go down to his local pub and find a group of like-minded individuals. He'd been a bit intimidated at first—being the only guy in a group of single women—but after a few rounds, he was able to let it go and have fun.

The first person to clink glasses with him took a reasoned swig of her Rekorderlig Passionfruit and smiled with the others. Olivia Dean was in the same situation as Farah, although for her it was Munzees instead of entomology. She spent the entire week leading up to tonight vacillating on whether she would actually attend; historically, she wasn't good in crowds. She'd only decided to meet with the rest of the group last night, and was pleasantly surprised that she was enjoying herself.

To her left sat Victoria Acton, the eldest of the bunch by nearly a decade. She was a successful graphic designer who owned her own company. Recently divorced, and quite messily, she was happy to be out and about again after twelve years of her façade of a marriage, even if it was something as low-key as this. She had forgotten how nice it was to be genuinely excited about something. She'd always been interested in ghosts, having grown up in an old house that had more than its fair share, but her brutal husband had cowed her to stop talking about it because she was "embarrassing herself." She had put up with her ex for so long because she thought there would be nothing worse than being alone, until the day she realized she was already alone in her own marriage. For the first time in a long time, she felt free to speak when and how she pleased.

Rounding out the table was Mia Davenport, the youngest of the group. She was still in university studying botany, although what she really wanted to be was a writer. None of the others knew it, but they were slowly making their way into her first novel; a story about a ghost doomed to wander forever until a group of plucky psychic investigators finally solves her centuries-old murder, allowing her spirit to pass on.

"Has anyone taken this tour before?" Davenport asked, referring to the ghost tour of Great Missenden.

"I have," Acton replied, "but it was nearly twenty years ago, so I don't know what to expect. I imagine a lot's changed." The rest replied in the negative.

"As the most haunted place in the Chilterns, it only seemed fitting to make it our initial group outing," Farah reasoned. Their online discussion had narrowed the area to the Chilterns, even though none of them were local to the area. It was unknown to them all and simply gorgeous—even if they didn't see any ghosts, they'd see some of the best scenery England had to offer. It also had geographical advantage, lying somewhat between all of their residences: St. Albans, Basingstoke, London, and Oxford.

They continued their conversation and were considering if there was time for another round while they waited for their tour guide, when an old woman approached their table and tentatively interrupted, "Hello, I am Vivienne Clark. Are you here for the tour?"

It took the foursome a second to register that the little old lady was referring to the tour they'd booked—dressed in a thick sweater, sensible trousers, and ochre hiking boots, she looked more suited to trekking than ghost hunting. "Yes! Yes, we are," Farah answered with a smile. "I'm Mo Farah, and this is Mia Davenport, Victoria Action, and Olivia Dean."

"We're the Chiltern Truth Seekers," Acton blurted out, feeling the need to explain why she was in the company of so many young people.

Clark smiled and shook their hands. "I haven't heard of that one," she responded.

"We're new—founded only a few months ago," Farah explained.

"That's nice," Clark remarked with complete sincerity. "Always glad to see young people interested in the old ways. Are you ready?"

With the remaining drinks quickly downed and the tab settled, the truth seekers were on High Street looking back at the Greysides. "Well, since we're already here, this is as good a place as any to start," Clark began.

"The Greysides was established in 1327 by William Glynd. It served as a coach inn for centuries, until the railway came in the mid-1800s. It has had several fires, but the most damaging one occurred in 1538, the same year that the abbey was dissolved—officially for economic reasons, but in reality for heresy and other misbehaviors. The timing worked out well for the Greysides; while the abbey church was being demolished and the stone salvaged for the nobility, the common villagers—equally angry with the abbey—decided to take all of the headstones from the abbey's graveyard and use them to rebuild their favorite inn. Incidentally, that is how the Greysides garnered its name."

"The entire place is covered in gravestones?!" Davenport exclaimed in horror, feeling a bit sickened. Of the group, she was the only religious one and the information elicited a guttural response from her; everyone else simply heard a cool fact about why a place could be haunted.

"More than three hundred and fifty gravestones were used to clad the Greysides, although some have been lost in repairs since then," Clark answered. "The stones were oriented so their smooth backsides faced outward and their faces against the walls. No one could tell their original purpose, because they looked no different than normal cut stone. Over time, people forgot all about where they came from.

"But the truth has a way of bubbling to the surface, and sometime in the late 1880s, one of the walls started sinking. Once they started removing stones during remediation, they realized all of them were gravestones, the epitaphs ironically well preserved because they had been spared 300 years of exposure. An extensive search of the parish records was conducted and the stones' origins uncovered."

"Gives a new meaning to recycling, doesn't it?" Farah quipped.

"It is *reuse*, reduce, recycle," Dean responded with a smirk.

Clark continued, "The discovery of the gravestones played a large role in the revitalization of interest in the supernatural here at Great Missenden. Even though the stories had continued to be told by the locals throughout the centuries, they weren't of larger interest. But once the Londoners heard of the building lined with defiled gravestones, it became fashionable for the well-to-do to hold séances at the Greysides. At the height of the craze, the upper parlor, now broken into three rooms, was holding nearly nightly séances."

"To any effect?" Dean asked.

"Oh yes! But unlike today's séances, those of that time were often filled with frauds, so it's hard to determine which were really contacting the other side and which weren't. However, there were multiple contacts with several of the same spirits over time. Clara Felton, a serving woman who hung herself when she became pregnant by a man who refused to acknowledge her, was the most-commonly contacted, but there were others. Johnathan Blake was another restless spirit commonly reached; he was an insurance broker who killed himself after going bankrupt when the *SS City of Glasgow* disappeared in the Atlantic. Then there were a mother and child, Elinor and Eva Livingstone, killed by their husband and father in a drunken rage.

"So much sadness and violence," Davenport quietly lamented.

"You can't make ghosts without breaking some eggs," Farah

joked.

"Quite right, Mr. Farah!" Clark responded. "And to borrow your turn of phrase, the few eggs broken here pale in comparison to the dozens cracked at the abbey over the years." She slipped into guide mode and pointed dramatically down the street to the darkness; the electric lights of the abbey cast deep shadows across the lane at oblique angles. "If you'll follow me, we'll see the heart of the matter."

The group followed her strident steps the quarter mile it took to stand before the abbey. She paused several times along the way, pointing out additional haunted locations—so many just off the main street—and everyone felt the tension build the closer they got to the ancient abbey. Once there, Clark began with a history of the abbey, from its founding in 1133 to its dissolution in 1538, but she kept it brief; her audience wasn't really interested in the normal history. They wanted the secret history.

"The abbey didn't become a problem for the church until a century after its founding. It was then that the first rumbles of heresy trickled out to the wider world. Some of the abbot's teachings conflicted with the official stance of the church, and the abbey was censored by having its abbot replaced by an Irish abbot, handpicked by the Pope himself.

"Things calmed down for a few years and the church seemed adequately appeased, but the seeds of discord were already sewn…by none other than the replacement abbot, who turned out to be even worse than his predecessor. Although he followed the tenants of the church in public, he was a heathen through and through. Soon the abbey was awash in paganism, but it was hidden from the common brother. The old ways went underground and were practiced in the cellars of the abbey and church."

"Old ways?" Farah interjected.

"The ways of the faerie, the ways of the wee ones."

"So he was putting out saucers of milk and such?" Acton commented with an unimpressed shrug.

"I don't know if he did that," the old lady responded. "But what I know he did do was human sacrifice."

That perked the group right up; human sacrifice at an Arrouaisian monastery—now that was exciting! Clark quickly followed up, noticing the spike in their interest, "Yes, human sacrifice. The abbot, named Conlaed, set up a sacrificial stone in the basement of the abbey church dedicated to the local fear dearg, which means 'red man' in Irish. The fear dearg—"

"I thought red men were just normal faeries," Davenport interrupted. "Mischievous, perhaps a bit cruel, but not bloodthirsty."

"Ah, we have someone with some knowledge," Clark smiled. "You're right, my dear; most faeries are playful, mischievous things, but not all of them. And this one, at least according to Abbot Conlaed, demanded human sacrifice to keep the monastery, the monks, and the abbot free from danger." Davenport found the explanation lacking, but Clark was determined to push forward—she wanted to give them their money's worth, but didn't want to be out here all night.

"So what happened?" Farrah nudged the tour forward; he wanted to get to the ghost part.

"Well, after several years, Conlaed was killed by the monks and thrown into a ditch, covered with only a thin layer of dirt. It is said his spirit roams the area, driven both by his quixotic quest for the next sacrifice to the fear dearg and the heinous nature of his death. He is better known now as the Black Monk, the most dangerous of all the spirits of Great Missenden."

*****

"So, what'd ya think?" Farah attempted to draw Davenport into conversation. She had grown quiet upon their return to the Greysides after the tour ended. Now it was just the two of them, Acton and Dean having made their exit a half hour ago, both wanting to catch their respective trains before their schedule slipped into running once every other hour. Farah had rented a room with the understanding that you never knew when you might want one, and Davenport had agreed to stay for another drink while the others set off. Her life was less time-sensitive, as she'd just finished the summer's first half-quarter and the second half-quarter didn't start until Monday.

"I thought it was interesting," she commented, sipping

her drink. "Vivienne seemed to know pretty much everything about everything."

"Well, she was probably there when it all happened!" Farah ribbed their guide.

Davenport smiled. "She definitely wasn't what I'd expected as a ghost tour host." She raised her hands, fluttered her fingers, and made a spooky "oOo!" noise. Her right eyebrow arched and she spoke conspiratorially, "Maybe she wasn't really there at all…maybe she was a ghost!"

That drew a laugh out of Farah. "Any self-respecting ghost wouldn't be caught dead in yellow hiking boots."

Davenport picked up her glass and tilted it in his direction. "Nice one, Mo, nice one." She finished her drink. "I think I'm going to go back to Oxford now."

"The night's still young," Farah argued.

Davenport looked up and down the dimly lit street. Nothing stirred. "The night may be young somewhere, but not here. It's going to take me an hour to get back—I'd rather not fall asleep on the train."

Farah shrugged to the inevitable. "At least let me walk you to the station. I've got credible local knowledge that this area is filled with dangerous sorts, of all kinds."

Davenport cracked up and her laughter was so authentic, it made Farah stand a little taller as he settled the bill—he had asked her to stay for a drink, after all. A chill had set in since their walking tour, and they set a quick pace along the deserted streets to the empty train station. They chattered about this and that for another half hour while they waited for her train. She gave him a friendly hug before boarding, and he stood by until the train was out of sight before leaving.

He knew it was just a goodbye hug, a sociable way to end the evening, but to him, it felt more like a beginning. He hadn't anticipated how hard it was simply to meet new people after he left uni, and tonight was the first time in a long time he felt normal. Maybe there were people who just might get him and his terrible puns—perhaps even appreciated them a bit. He knew he couldn't read people worth shit, and the last thing he wanted to do was blow things out of proportion—a hug is just a hug. *But what the hell*, he thought as he turned the corner onto High Street and turned off his constant internal analysis. *Might as well enjoy the feeling while you have it.* He was all alone: it was okay to let himself get excited at possibilities.

Farah tucked his head down and walked rapidly, trying to regain a measure of the warmth he'd lost waiting for the train. He should have been paying more attention when he changed direction instead of focusing on grand romantic fictions about a woman he'd just met, but such is the way of youth. His lack of awareness didn't bother the steel lamppost that Farah unwittingly collided into. It hit with a resonant thud against the right side of his forehead. As he fell back to the ground, the other side of his head impacted against the concrete. Farah watched the world spin into a mix of blurred lights and then fell into darkness.

When he regained consciousness moments later, he gingerly touched his forehead, wincing at the pain. His fingers returned covered in blood. Rising unsteadily, he left three long crimson smudges down the lamppost. The streetlights softly hummed and the crickets chirped, oblivious to what had happened. He took a few tentative steps before finally finding most of his balance again.

Farah grunted in pain as he checked the other side of his head and again discovered blood. Wiping it off on his chest, he took a few more steps, but listed to his right. Struggling to stay upright, he leaned against a nearby shop wall until he felt ready to continue, but when he finally launched himself off the wall, he found that he wasn't all right. The world didn't quite seem level.

Over the next five minutes he tried again and again, but each time he leaned, stumbled, and found himself against the cold wall. *I gotta call an ambulance*, he hazily thought. *Something's messed up.* He reached into his back pocket, pulled out his phone, and dialed 999. It rang twice before connecting.

"Hello, emergency services," a crisp female voice responded. "Which service do you require?"

"I've fallen and busted my head. I can't walk straight," Farah eked out. He found it hard to speak, like there was taffy in his mouth.

"I'll connect you to ambulance services," the voice quickly

replied.

Farah waited for the transfer, but it never came. Eventually he looked at his phone and saw he wasn't connected anymore. He dialed 999 again. "Hello, emergency services," a male voice answered this time.

"I've hurt my head and I need…" The phone cut out before he could finish. He looked down at the phone. *What the hell?*

The crickets stopped chirping. A solemn timbre filled the night, "No, no. That won't do."

Farah spun his head to look at the speaker and immediately regretted it. He started vomiting and in his state, fought hard to not fall into his own sick, which made him hurl harder. After a final empty heave, he wiped his mouth with his left hand and slid his phone into the front pocket of his pants with his other hand. Only then did Farah *slowly* turn his head to the speaker.

A pale man stood a few feet away. He was clad in dark robes with a hood that was pulled back, displaying a crisp tonsure. He held his pasty hand out to Farah. "Come brother, there is something I *must* show you."

Chapter Six

Danbury, Connecticut, USA
28th of June, 1:30 a.m. (GMT-4)

Wilson walked down the empty street; a cheap pawnshop leather briefcase silently swaying in his hand. All the houses he passed were still, all trussed up for the summer night. A few had open windows, but most were closed against the night's low. Without warning, he disappeared from street view as he dashed between two houses and crouched in the shadow of one of the buildings. He paused and listened—blessed silence. He quickly rummaged through his briefcase, pulling out a very short, knotted rope with a padded grappling hook on its end. Wilson stood and swung it about, launching it to the second-floor balcony of the Western Connecticut Paranormal Society. It landed with a palpable thud and he pulled the slack, securing it against the solid brick half-wall that functioned as the balcony's railing. Once he was sure it was set, he tied the briefcase to the loose end of the rope.

Wilson hurriedly climbed up, pulled up briefcase behind him, and retrieved the night vision goggles from the case while he tucked the grapple and rope back into place in one smooth motion. Goggles on, he inspected the balcony door's lock—it wouldn't be difficult to open with the picks in his case, but it was barred from within. Wilson moved on to the windows, which still had the tale-tell red lights that he had seen in the back windows. While technically functioning, they were no longer connected to Independent Alarm and Security's system—the signal was dead in the water.

Like many older houses in northern climes, the windows had been replaced with tasteful faux-wooden framed vinyl windows that had an exploitable design flaw—repeatedly rocking them up and down in their hinges could release the sliding locks, and eventually the window would come out of its casing when the sash stops popped under variable pressure. Everyone knew about the flaw, but they just didn't see it as such—they only saw an easy way of removing the window to make exterior cleaning simple. But that was the nature of security; anything that made life easier, made security harder.

Wilson softly swayed the window on its hinge for several minutes before it gave, falling out of its casing. Cradling it in his arms, he turned it until the lock fully released. He set the window down on the interior and shimmied through the window frame. Then he paused for a two-minute listen—his standard practice when he infiltrated without a time restraint. Two minutes of silence and stillness was just long enough for someone to return to sleep if they were roused, or lose interest if they were already awake, typically convincing themselves that they were hearing things or the house was just settling. There shouldn't be anyone here at this time of night, but practicing good tradecraft was its own reward.

Once he was sure that he hadn't roused anyone, Wilson silently went to work. He first replaced the window, leaving it unlocked, and then went up a floor into the converted attic where he knew the *A Bump in the Night* crew did all of their video analysis. He'd eventually go through every room in the house, but he wanted to start at the top and hit their main pile of equipment first.

Wilson produced two large brick-like objects from his case. The first was an electromagnet that could be plugged into a wall socket. The second was an EMP generator draped in a large piece of Faraday fabric. He methodically processed every electronic device he could find, blasting it first with a powerful magnetic field and then following up with a localized EMP burst contained within the Faraday fabric—it took more effort, but he preferred precision when he had the luxury of time. After all, an indiscriminate EMP would also affect all of his electronics and make it harder to disguise his work.

Using this technique, it took more than half an hour to do the analysis room, and Wilson was glad he'd started an hour earlier than he'd originally considered when he finally moved to the other rooms. Between all the kit used in the show and the security system, he had pegged the WCPS as tech-junkies, but what he found was beyond the pale. It took him another two hours spent completely bricking all the rest of the electronics in the house, some of which he knew were decades old and probably didn't work anyway, but he had to make sure.

Once everything was dead, he scrambled all the CDs he could find using a UV-based, rapid laser light data destroyer. It was unlikely that the footage was on a CD, and there weren't very many of them, but Wilson was nothing if not a thorough man. Besides, he was making the world a better place by destroying an old copy of...*Baby One More Time*, by his reckoning. Once all the CDs were nuked, he cracked the safe he'd found in the closet of one of the second-story rooms. It contained papers, cash, some gold and platinum bullion, and a memory stick, which he wiped before setting it back inside.

It was now a little past four, and he was going to lose the darkness soon. He descended to the unfinished basement—his final stop—where he tripped every circuit breaker, creating the illusion of a power surge that broke through the safeguards in place. With everything completed inside, Wilson shimmied out the window and jiggled it until the lock slid back enough to appear as if someone had just failed to turn it all the way—the mind had an uncanny knack of filling in the blanks with reasonable solutions.

He removed his suit from the briefcase, changed into his normal clothes, and launched himself over the balcony wall, gracefully falling to the ground with a roll. He reemerged from between the homes and sauntered to his car. Halfway there, he started concentrating—*think, think, think*—on the utility pole at the end of the street. By the time Wilson opened the door to his car, the distribution transformer atop the pole couldn't take the heat anymore and burst into flames, knocking out the power for the whole neighborhood.

The rush from conjuring energy wasn't nearly as potent as when he dominated another's will with magic, but it was substantial enough that it would take a few hours for him to come down and make sleep possible. Wilson drove away through the unlit streets of his target neighborhood and pulled into a local diner for a plain breakfast of eggs, bacon, and toast, sans coffee—he needed to catch a *few* hours of sleep before his flight to the UK tonight. The waitress who took his order didn't know why the gentleman in the booth looked so pleased, but it was a rarity these days, especially this early in the morning. *Good for him; the world needs more happy people*, she thought as she brought his orange juice with a smile.

As Wilson waited for his food, he thumbed out a message to the Salt Mine: *MA–summon the cloud scrubbers*. To UK tonight. It wouldn't surprise him if WCPS backed up their data in the cloud, but now that he'd destroyed the local data center, his part was done. It was up to the Mine's hackers to make sure there weren't any digital copies floating around. There was always the possibility of a physical backup at a secondary location—stored in a personal residence or safety deposit box—but in his experience, people rarely had the discipline to perform regular and frequent backups that were protocol in professional sectors, and no exterior data storage company was listed as a deduction in their audit. The Salt Mine would keep its ear to the ground, but that wasn't his concern right now—he was off to the green hills of England.

He was still grinning from ear to ear when his food arrived. The waitress had made a little smiley face out of the eggs and bacon, and he noticed she had a nice-looking sway as she walked to the other side of the restaurant to take the order of another early bird diner. Thoughts percolated, but Wilson tamped them down—*never let the magic do the thinking*.

Chapter Seven

Aylesbury, Buckinghamshire, UK
29th of June, 4:55 a.m. (GMT+1)

Detective Chief Inspector Jones woke to the incessant buzz of his phone—his was not a job where you could turn off your mobile for the night. With a quick glance at the clock on the bedside table, he surmised that it wouldn't be good news.

"This is Jones," he answered groggily. His wife rolled over, vainly trying to block out the conversation.

The voice of Detective Constable Tull was on the other end, "We've got a body. Abbey Park, Great Missenden. It's ugly."

"I'll be there in half an hour," Jones said before hanging up.

"Do be careful," his wife mumbled before he rolled out of bed.

He turned back and kissed her head. "Always."

He dressed rapidly with an efficiency and grace acquired from an early age and reinforced in the course of his profession, and in less than ten minutes, DCI Jones was out the door. A considerate man, he waited until he was on the A413 before turning on his lights—no need to disturb the neighbors. Fifteen minutes later, he pulled up next to three other police vehicles along High Street, opposite the park. One of them was the coroner's transit.

Abbey Park was the name given to the eight plus acres of land south of the Great Missenden Abbey after its dissolution. It was one of the few places in Buckinghamshire with large, majestic trees; most of the old growth had been cut down in the nineteenth century to feed the local furniture industry. Technically, the River Misbourne flowed through the park, but it was unpredictably intermittent, disappearing for several years last decade. It was flowing this year, but it was so narrow that if a tall man fell in ass-first, he could still have a dry head and dry feet.

Jones had visited the park once before in his official capacity, but he didn't get to see very much of it. It had been a fundraiser, and he'd spent most of his time in the dunk tank, allowing local teens a chance to dunk an officer for a pound. From what he remembered, it was a long triangular park with its point facing south.

DC Tull was waiting for him as soon as he got out. Tull was a big man, trim and athletic. He was just over a year out of graduation, but coming along nicely. "Victim is one Muhammad Farah, age twenty-four, no priors. He was found by a jogger around 4:30 this morning."

"The Olympian?"

"No sir," Tull answered, handing over the coffee he'd gotten for his DCI. He started down a small path leading into the park and Jones followed. "This Mo Farah is a programmer for the Royal Entomological Society…insects—"

"I know what entomological means, Tully," Jones snapped.

"Sorry, sir."

"Twenty-four? Seems a bit young for the position," Jones puzzled.

"From the records we've gotten so far, Farah seems to have been educated in both computer science and entomology at the University of Reading."

"Ah, not a common crossover, I expect; probably made him a prime candidate right out of school."

"I would assume so," Tull replied. As they came out of the trees into the large field that composed most of the park, he warned his DCI, "Prepare yourself."

Jones could see the crime scene about a hundred yards away, just on the other side of a massive old ash tree adjacent to the thin Misbourne. The sun was burning off the low hazy clouds of the morning, sending the dew-laden grass into scintillating color. It was beautiful, and Jones felt his chest compact, as it so often did when he approached a life snuffed out. They followed the path, crossed a small footbridge, and swung around the ash, revealing the officers and coroner standing near the corpse of Mr. Farah.

He was in a sitting position, back to the tree, and clothed only below the waist. The entire torso above the waist had been skinned, leaving behind only muscle and small deposits of fat. The corpse's skin remained on both of its arms and on its neck and head, but everything else was flayed.

"Bloody hell," Jones uncharacteristically uttered.

"My thoughts exactly, DCI Jones," the coroner replied in greeting. Mr. Hugo Mereworth was a portly, tired-looking young man who'd taken his position for the money. Jones didn't like him, but worked with him as well as he'd worked with the past coroner, whose untimely demise half a year ago was still somewhat of a mystery. It'd looked like a murder-suicide, and had been ruled as such, but that explanation didn't sit well with Jones.

"How's the jogger?" Jones inquired, his mind immediately concerned with the welfare of the living.

Mereworth pointed further down the path, where an officer sat with a young woman on a bench facing the Misbourne. "She's shaken, but seems to be dealing as well as could be expected.

Jones walked around the corpse. "Not nearly enough blood; looks like a dump."

"We're getting the local camera info on the two roads abutting the park," Tull spoke, preempting the DCI's request.

Jones grunted, slipped on some gloves, and examined the body. "Rather serious impact on the right side of the head."

"Knocked out?"

"Possibly. I don't think Mr. Farah would have cooperated, and as there's no ligature marks, it's a reasonable assumption." He continued probing. "Another impact on the back of the head." He flipped the head back and forth. "Looks to be almost opposite the first impact."

"Somebody hit him twice?" Tull postulated. "Once in the front and then the second running away?"

"Maybe. It could have been two attackers, however. If it was a single assailant, it would imply a left-hander." Finished with the corpse's head, Jones moved downward. "Phone located in front right trouser pocket," he declared to Tull, who wrote down the information. "Seems to still be working. If the phone's still in his pocket, how did we identify him?"

"His wallet was found near his feet," Mereworth answered.

"We'll get the phone records, sir," Tull said, opening an evidence bag for the phone. "No blood on the phone, either. Why would you do this and not destroy the phone?"

"Good question, Tully. Who *would* take the time to do this—and it did take time—only to leave the phone behind and a wallet right next to him? Why not destroy them or throw them into the river half a mile away where there'd be chance that they wouldn't be found, at least not right away?"

"Better still would be to ditch the phone after grabbing Mr. Farah so we wouldn't be able to determine where the grab occurred, and then drop the wallet somewhere else entirely," Tull ventured.

"Precisely. Everyone knows you can track people by their phones now. Make a note for forensics to carefully examine if the phone or the wallet has been tampered with to deliberately lead us astray," Jones ordered. "I prefer my killers to be stupid, but I'm not going to assume it." He continued examining the corpse. "What's this on the left wrist?"

Tull looked down, as did the coroner. "Can't tell, sir."

"Looks like dried snot. Or vomit?" offered Mereworth. "Lord knows I've seen enough over the past three months." Mereworth's wife had just had triplets.

Jones called over one of the technicians; he felt confident in his ability to bag a phone, but biological material was best left in the hands of the well trained. He stood up, disposed of his gloves, and waited until the tech finished scraping the material into a sterile container. They'd do a whole battery of tests once they got the body to the morgue.

"Well, that looks like it, gentlemen," DCI Jones declared. "It's all yours, Mr. Mereworth. Once you're done, we'll clear the scene and re-open the park." He looked at Tull, "Breakfast?"

Chapter Eight

London, UK
29th of June, 9:10 a.m. (GMT+1)

The plane's wheels touched down on the ground, and the subsequent shudder of the landing roused Wilson from his sleep. He was momentarily confused about where and when he was, but quickly regained his bearings. Pushing up the window, he peered out onto the bustling Heathrow tarmac in the morning's light. He checked his Girard-Perregaux for local time and did some math, amazed that he had slept for a full six hours. Normally he couldn't sleep on flights, and it wasn't from a lack of trying on his numerous trips; catching an hour was about the best he could normally do. *Must have been the window seat*, he thought as he debouched the plane—it was a rare treat, as his plane tickets for work were often bought on little notice, leaving him with the seats no one else wanted.

In half an hour, he was on the road in his rental—a nondescript blue Vauxhall Corsa—and another half hour brought him to the Greysides, his hotel for the duration of his stay in the UK and the watering hole for the ghostly inclined in Great Missenden. Three stories tall, the ground floor was a pub-slash-restaurant with twelve guest rooms on the second story. The third floor was a half-story, containing the private residence of the owners that were originally rooms for those in service, back in the day.

It had been nearly a decade since Wilson's first stay at the hotel, when he'd brokered a continuation of the 1917 Pacification Treaty with the ghostly populace of the isle. Under the accord, the ghosts promised to leave the living uninjured in exchange for weekly ritualistic tributes throughout the country, organized by the Salt Mine at key locations for maximum coverage. Great Missenden featured heavily in the compromise due to two factors: the mobility of spirits and magical geography.

Contrary to myth, ghosts were quite mobile, able to move miles away from where they were formed. This knowledge of ghostly movement was easily overlooked, even among practitioners of the arts. After all, when all the sightings and séances of a ghost appear in a particular area and nowhere else, it was natural to assume that the ghost "lived" there and was bound to its respective areas. Even the majority of mediums did not know that ghosts could travel—mostly because they were frauds, but even the genuine ones found it difficult to speak with traveling ghosts because the locals would muscle past them to have a chat. It wasn't impossible to speak to travelers, but there were few ghosts powerful enough to make their presence known out of their home territory. It was a matter of power—the farther away a ghost moved from its formation area, the weaker it was.

If a ley line happened to be within a ghost's mobility radius, it could travel along the line and any other lines it was connected to, like supernatural transit. Due to a conflux of ley lines that formed a great star, centered on the abbey, Great Missenden was the magical bellybutton of the isle and consequently the hottest part of the country for real ghost activity. The rituals held there were vital to maintain the appeasement of the spirits, which made an apparent ghost attack on Gemma Green concerning.

Wilson entered the Greysides, carefully rolling his luggage after him. The interior was the picture-perfect English country inn, and a perky young man enthusiastically greeted him at the check-in counter, "Welcome to the Greysides! Checking in?"

"Yes. You should have a reservation for a Mr. Warwick," Wilson spoke evenly.

"Ah, Mr. Warwick! Yes, we have you for a very early check in. Your room is the Grand Turret." The receptionist cheerily handed over the door key cards, provided the WiFi information, and explained how to get to his room. Wilson trudged up the stairs to his large corner suite with a circular bartizan turret facing the abbey. The nook was filled by a small circular table and trio of chairs—perfect for a quiet and relaxing breakfast.

He wasted no time unpacking and once everything was in order, strolled down High Street in search of the Roald Dahl museum. Opposite the museum was a small cobblestoned path onto which he turned. The sun rarely touched the ground in the alley, and a thin layer of green moss grew in the cracks of the stones. Tucked beneath the boughs of a trio of leafy trees at the end of the lane stood his destination: the house of Ms. Vivienne Clark.

Clark was an employee of the Institute of Tradition—another front organization of the Salt Mine—and had been for decades, according to her file. They'd recruited her almost forty years ago to perform weekly and seasonal rituals, designed to placate the ghosts that claimed Great Missenden as their home as well as those who visited. In exchange, the Institute paid her a few thousand pounds per month, providing her complete financial freedom to pursue her artistic desires. She was not a magician, a psychic, or anything special; she was an ordinary person who just happened to have an extraordinary task. However, she did know there were those who practiced magic, and her experience with the paranormal was significantly greater than the average person.

Her house was at least three hundred years, but it was well maintained. A newish slate roof covered the ancient beams, and the thick cob walls featured a new coat of plaster and paint—a pale pink below the prominent tarred mid-beam that circumscribed the house, and a delicate blue above. Pastel figures, flourishes, vignettes in green, red, and white randomly graced the exterior wall, capturing the whimsy and whim of the artist as inspiration came, without regard to topic, theme, or style.

This had been Clark's home ever since taking the job with the Institute. While rituals and tours paid the bills, in her heart, she was an artist and the world her canvas. Her reasoning was as follows: a house needed a fresh coat of paint every couple of years, so why not make it artful? She followed her muse, and once her canvas was full, it was time for a fresh base coat to capture the next spark.

Wilson knocked on the door—a thick reclaimed thing—and was happy to find Clark at home. Normally, he would have called and set up a meeting, but catching her unaware was part of his assessment—people could mask and compensate for slipping mental faculties with enough notice and preparation. As he waited for a response, he admired a partially filled milk saucer in front of the door. It was shaped like a cow and bore the name "Mr. Fiddles."

The sound of wood-on-wood revealed a small gap, and a voice came through the old-fashioned sliding peephole. "Hello," Clark greeted him.

Wilson took a step back so she could see more of him before speaking. "Ms. Clark, I'm Damon Warwick from the Institute of Tradition. I don't know if you remember me, but we've met before, about a decade ago, when I was here to secure a continuation of the Treaty of Great Missenden. I'd like to speak with you a bit today, if possible." He waited patiently for a reply, standing tall with his arms at his sides. Eventually, the peephole slid closed, and Wilson heard the sound of the door unlocking. It swung open, revealing its full four inches of thickness in profile.

"Mr. Warwick, so nice to see you again," Clark warmly welcomed him with a wave of her arm. "Do come in and have a seat. I'll put the kettle on. Mind the cat's saucer."

Wilson entered, closing the heavy door behind him, and took a seat on a couch of disreputable manufacture covered by a thick throw that concealed all but its outline. The interior of the house coordinated with its exterior, if you accepted the premise that chaos could be matched with chaos. The clash of shapes, colors, textures, and materials made Wilson feel like he was inside an art instillation rather than a sitting room, and Wilson was not a connoisseur of modern art.

A hodge-podge of decor filled every nook, and it looked much the same as it had since his last visit, with the notable addition of the heavily scratched red Kit-Cat clock with a broken tail—taped together, of course. Superficially, there appeared to be no plan or artistic vision beyond "this object pleases me," but his keen eye noticed that nothing was out of place. Everything *felt* like it was where it belonged, and importantly, everything was dusted. The haphazard nature was one that was deliberately chosen and cultivated, presumably to elicit an emotional reaction—wasn't that the point of art? Wilson would never say as much, but the only urge it evoked in him was the desire to declutter.

Wilson heard the kettle go off, and Clark entered the

room soon after, carrying a tray with two cups, six small tins of various teas, and all the accoutrements—a silver sugar cube holder, matching tongs, a tiny cream pitcher, and two stainless steel tea infusers shaped like dolphins. She carefully set the tray in front of him and named each of the teas on offer. They were all loose leaf and without much thought, he picked a gunpowder Lapsang Souchong; Clark's small smile flagged her approval at his selection. Only after the tea was seeping did she venture into conversation, "So Mr. Warwick, to what do I owe the pleasure?"

Wilson broke from his typical impassive mien, conveying cordial intent with his body language and a slight smile. "As you know, we at the Institute of Tradition are deeply concerned with the wellbeing and safety of every member of Great Britain, living or deceased. It is our utmost goal to see that the old ways are followed and that peace between the living and the dead remains in blessed existence."

"Yes, of course," she heartily agreed.

"And it is this desire which has led me to your door," he delicately broached the subject of her duties.

"Word sure travels fast among your kind, Mr. Warwick," she commented obliquely. "You think the murder has something to do with the spirit folk?"

"Murder?" Wilson asked.

"So you *don't* know," Clark surmised with a gleam in her eyes. "Tea's ready," she announced. She served his with a single cube of demerara and dressed her dark Assam with equal parts cream and sugar. She reverently took a sip and Wilson followed her cue—clearly there would be no more conversation until their teas were deemed satisfactory. Wilson's was perfect; whatever one could say about Clark's decorating skills, she had a fine choice of teas.

"What were we talking about?" She came out of her tea-induced reverie. "Ah, yes, the murder. The whole town is talking about it. Happened sometime last night, and the body was just removed a few hours ago."

"In Great Missenden?" Wilson verified.

"Indeed, just down the street in Abbey Park."

Wilson's stomach sank; if the WCPS job hadn't taken an extra day to execute, he could have been here before the murder occurred, when he was just looking into an assault. An isolated injury to the living could be written off as the reprehensible action of an errant spirit; it had happened two other times since the original signing of the treaty, and reparations and amendments were reached to keep the peace.

But murder was entirely different. It was an unpardonable escalation in spirit aggression that could rightfully raise the full ire of the Salt Mine, something that would put the entire spirit community on edge. The Treaty of Great Missenden wasn't just for the protection of the living; there were stipulations that safeguarded the ghosts from the dangers of the living—namely practitioners of the arts. Experienced magicians could capture ghosts and bind them into pre-existing talismans or mundane objects to create a new magical item. These items were much less costly in karma, as the item fed off the ghost's residual energy, acting like a battery of sorts.

Clark read the dark look that came over Wilson's face and saw that she was not bearing good news, but waited for him to speak. She took a deliberately long sip of tea, giving him time to gather his thoughts.

"No, we weren't aware of the murder, but I'm afraid it could be ghostly in nature," Wilson broke the silence candidly.

"I don't understand why you would think that," she tersely replied.

"There was an actress injured a little over a week ago—"

"Her?" Clark indigently tutted. "She's just another attention seeker desperate to see her name in the paper."

Wilson put his cup and saucer on the tray. "We have reason to believe otherwise, at least enough to do a full investigation." That brought her up short. "I hate to be rude, but I'd like to see your journal, as well as watch you perform the weekly rituals," Wilson requested.

"Ah. You think I may have failed, and you want to test me before you approach the others," she wagered a guess. She remained dignified despite the inherent insult such an inquiry bore. One of the requirements of her position was a yearly observation to confirm she was still performing the primary ritual as required. Every few years, a more detailed assessment was taken regarding the special seasonal rituals. To her knowledge, she had never been found lacking in nigh forty years—a fact known to Wilson, who had reviewed her file extensively before he came.

Wilson could see she was offended, even though she hid it well. "Precisely," Wilson agreed gently. "We have to start looking at the site of the attack."

"Well then, Mr. Warwick, shall we adjourn to the shed?" She rose and started toward the back of the house. It was one of those questions that was an order.

Wilson followed the elderly woman through the house, which was decorated in much the same fashion as the parlor—nothing matched anything else, but it somehow all belonged together. The back door, like the front, was obviously reclaimed from another structure; its brass locks and porthole suggested a ship of some kind. The backyard was large by UK standards and filled with plants vegetative, herbal—and if Wilson's eyes weren't failing—illegal.

As a general rule, the British took their sheds seriously—a far departure from the rickety thing set aside to hold dusty and cobwebbed tools—and Clark was no exception. Like the house, the shed was made of cob and occupied the northwestern corner of the lot. It was easily four hundred square feet and decorated with the same freewheeling style as the house. Clark held the door open for Wilson, and much to his surprise, he found immaculate order within. On one shelf were all the dried herbs that the rituals required, arranged alphabetically. On the one below, the collection of oils, again, arranged alphabetically. The main part of the shed was given over to a dais composed of interlocking slabs of slate. It was ground and polished to such perfection that it reflected, like a black pool of still water. Against the only wall devoid of storage shelves was a rigid Georgian oak bench in remarkable condition.

Seeing this magnificent display of standardization, Wilson doubted that Clark had failed to perform her duties. It was the diametric opposite of the rest of Clark's space and suggested she consciously embraced spontaneity and chaos—that all the whimsy of the main house was merely a counterbalance for the regulation and structure of the shed.

Clark motioned for Wilson to sit and he did as commanded, sliding onto the bench into the small depressions created by over more than two centuries of use. She retrieved a leather-bound book from an antique iron safe and handed it to him. "This is my ledger. It is a record of everything I have done for the Institute of Tradition during the past thirty-eight years."

Wilson opened the book as she gathered the materials needed for the weekly ritual. A quick perusal showed that, year after year, she'd performed every ritual required of her, a total of nearly eighty per year. Each entry was written in ink using a fountain pen and meticulously contained a complete list of ingredients used. The color of the ink changed each year, creating a rainbow effect when he flipped through the pages to check the latest entries. She did not appear to be remiss in her recent requirements, provided that the record wasn't simply a methodical lie. Wilson closed the book, placed it on the bench, and silently waited. It would take a while for her to prepare everything.

"You're not the talkative type," Clark noted as she retrieved one of the three oils she'd need and placed it on the modified apothecary shelf adjacent to the slate dais. Each slot of the shelf had several labels, which Wilson knew contained a list of ingredients for the common rituals, even though he could not read them from this distance. Even her organization was designed for optimal outcomes.

"No, I am not," Wilson concurred with her assessment.

"You're a magician, aren't you?" she asked, even though she knew the answer.

"I am," he answered warily.

"Good," she replied, as she stilled her hands briefly and turned around to look Wilson in the eye. "Then I will ask you a question, something that has worried me, but something I haven't spoken of to anyone else. I am old, yes?" She held her wrinkled hands before her. "But I do not feel old. I have no aches nor pains that others of my age have." She paused for a moment and turned away from Wilson and back to her work. She put up the last of her ingredients as her question rushed forward, "Has what I've been doing all these years done something to me?"

Wilson stood and approached. He squatted down to where she sat on a pillow next to the apothecary shelves. "May I see your hands?"

She looked surprised at his request, but offered him both of her hands. Wilson took them in his and turned her palms upward. He stared at them for a while and then asked, "When you are done with the weekly ritual, how to you feel?"

"Refreshed," she spoke without hesitation. "Always refreshed."

"Have you ever felt bad after one of the seasonal rituals?"

She almost spoke, but then stopped and closed her eyes. "Only once." The response was filled with a heavy sadness.

"And this was when your husband was still alive, no? And when you were much younger? When your children were still children?"

"Yes," she responded. Wilson saw the tears forming in her eyes.

"Then you know why," he said, releasing her hands.

"After all this time?"

Wilson nodded. "Yes, after all this time. She's still here, the little one that passed. She wishes you well, and so you are well. It is a blessing, of sorts."

Clark wiped the side of her face and formed a haunted smile, the kind that Wilson had all too often seen on his own face. Even though she wasn't a magician, she and he were alike in that one way— the price was often paid in unknown ways and at unknown times. When it was finally discovered, there was naught to do but smile.

Chapter Nine

Aylesbury, Buckinghamshire, UK
29th of June, 11:45 a.m. (GMT+1)

"I'll be there," DCI Jones affirmed before ending the call. He slipped his mobile back into his pocket and popped his head out of his office. "Let's go, Tully."

Tull, who was in the middle of a call, placed his hand over the mouthpiece before asking, "Where to?"

Jones put his jacket on and grabbed his keys. "Slough morgue. That was Dr. Brinston. He wants to talk to me." The last time Jones had gotten such a call was regarding the Grollo case, which turned out to be the strangest he had ever worked. He didn't typically take his DC along, but it was time for Tull to broaden his horizons.

Tull nodded and followed suit, abruptly making his apologies to the party on the other end of the line. On the drive, he filled in Jones on the new information they'd acquired. "Phone records show that Mr. Farah was out for the inaugural meeting of the 'Chiltern Truth Seekers' with three others—"

"Chiltern Truth Seekers?" Jones queried.

"Yes sir, a society that Mr. Farah had just founded a few months earlier—ghost hunters," Tull responded, his voice as nonjudgmental as he could muster.

"Ah," Jones matched his DC's tone.

"Precisely, sir. The others of the group are: Mia Davenport, age twenty-one, biology student and resident at Oxford; Victoria Acton, age thirty-six, owner of Acton Action Graphics and resident of West Brompton; and Olivia Dean, age twenty-seven, programmer at Fujitsu and resident of Basingstoke. We haven't been able to track down more than the basics for the last two; they haven't returned our calls."

Jones kept his eyes on the road but that didn't stop the gears from turning in his head. He didn't like the unreturned calls—in this day and age of instantaneous communication, it sent up a warning bell. "What do we know about the first one?"

Tull flipped to a new page of his notebook. "Mia Davenport. I was just wrapping up with her on the phone before we left. She said the group was there to meet and take a haunted tour, led by a Vivienne Clark, age seventy-one, an artist of some sort. Clark is a bit of a fixture in the area, running ghost tours for decades, and has been a resident of Greater Missenden her whole life."

Jones said nothing while maneuvering the car around one of the many hills between Aylesbury and Slough. Tull paused his narrative to allow his DCI to focus on the road. Once around the bend, Tull continued, "According to Davenport, the four of them met at the Greysides Inn in the early evening and had a long dinner followed by several rounds of drinks before setting off on the tour, sometime around eleven at night. She guessed the tour lasted for about an hour, after which they went back to the Greysides and had a few more rounds. Acton and Dean left—via train—around one o'clock this morning, and Davenport followed about an hour later. Farah walked her to the station, and she caught the 2:15 back to Oxford."

"So no one knows what Farah did between 2:15 and 4:30?" Jones checked his mental account.

"Correct, sir, but according to Davenport, Farah had rented a room at the Greysides," Tull added.

"Good to know. First, let's make sure he checked in, and then we'll need to take a look at his room and go through his belongings. Any response on the request for video from the park-side cameras?"

"They're saying I should get the files sometime between one and two this afternoon," Tull answered as he added items to his to-do list.

"Good. We need to expand our camera request now that we have an idea of where Farah was besides being at the park. Get the images from the train station as well as the nearby cameras oriented to capture foot-traffic between the station and Greysides. If we're lucky, we'll be able to track him as he goes."

They rode in silence for a bit before Tull quietly spoke. "I've got a bad feeling about this one, like the one I had with Grollo."

Jones didn't immediately respond but eventually admitted, "Me too, Tully. Me too."

****

Slough Hospital was one of many public buildings erected in the 1960s, and it looked it. Constructed of gray concrete and gray steel—now rusting in several locations—it embodied the brutalist style so popular at the time. A post-modern monolith punctuated with gray windows, it loomed over the neighborhood like Quasimodo among a gaggle of well-dressed children.

DCI Jones and DC Tull had an appointment with Dr. Andrew Brinston, the medical examiner at Slough, where the body of the deceased Mr. Muhammad Farah has been sent earlier in the day. Brinston could be a prickly fellow, but he was sharp as a tack and had considerable pull in the area's medical community. As such, Jones took great pains to remain on Brinston's good side. Over the years of working together, the rough edges in their professional interactions had been ground down, and they had developed a good rapport despite Brinston's quirks.

The neutral-yet-antiseptic smell endemic to all medical facilities hit Jones and Tull as they entered the hospital and roamed the maze of corridors that led to the morgue. After a short brisk minute walk, they showed their IDs to the single guard on duty and headed downstairs into the basement. Jones steadied himself before pushing the swinging double doors open—he was not a fan of this part of his job.

The hinges were still squeaking when Brinston called out, "Ah, DCI Jones, right on time as normal." His voice had a quality of absentmindedness, a dilly-dallying timbre that rose and fell like the cadence of a man who'd forgotten where he put his keys, even when he was elbow-deep in gore. Brinston was a tall, thin man with close-cut brown hair that circled his head, and the bright full-spectrum lights reflected off his smooth pate. He was bent over the corpse of Farah, needle and thread in hand. "If you'll wait just a moment, I'll be right with you."

Jones and Tull stepped toward the steel table, and Brinston glanced up at their approach. "I see you brought someone with you. DC Tull, is it?"

"Yes, sir," Tull replied.

"Nice to see you again, DC Tull. It's important that you familiarize yourself with all aspects of the work," Brinston espoused his thoughts while his fingers executed the stitches on muscle memory. "I do wish that DCI Jones would bring you every time he visited."

"As do I, sir," Tull politely agreed with Brinston, diplomatically flashing a "sorry, boss" look Jones's way.

"And there we go," Brinston announced as he tied off the last knot. He replaced his materials on the nearby cart and stood to his full height. "So, Mr. Muhammad Farah; where to begin?"

"Cause of death, if you would," Jones suggested. This was a well-orchestrated chess match that Jones and Brinston had played many times, and Jones opened with his typical gambit—come at it directly and test how oblique Brinston was feeling today.

With a straight face, Brinston answered, "Blood loss." Dr. Brinston was parsimonious with direct answers when he had the luxury of walking "his investigators" through the process. How else would the detectives of the Criminal Investigation Department even learn? He had an unfailing confidence in the importance of education, and each corpse that landed on his table was a teaching moment.

Jones maintained his game face and looked thoughtfully at Mr. Farah. "Okay," he acknowledged his opponent's move. "The obvious source of blood loss would be the removed skin on the torso, but I seriously doubt it was consensual. The lack of ligature marks suggests he was otherwise subdued. So my next questions are 'Any drugs in his system that could produce unconsciousness?' and 'Were the head wounds enough to produce such?'" Jones had become accustomed to this educational treatment and had grown to enjoy it. It was definitely better than reading about forensics, which was drier than a Sauvignon Blanc.

"Excellent questions, DCI," Brinston praised him. "There was only alcohol in Mr. Farah's system, and not enough to cause unconsciousness. For his weight, age and gender, my guess is no more than a few drinks were consumed prior to death. As to the head wounds, they appear superficial, although other information—"

"What information?" Tull interrupted abruptly. Jones shot him a look, and Tull immediately knew he had made a faux pas, but wasn't entirely sure how to fix. He opted for adding "Dr. Brinston" to the end of his question.

"The vomit on his left hand, Tull," Brinston stated flatly. Jones hoped he wasn't the only one that picked up on the lack of honorific in Brinston's response. Tull nodded obsequiously, and Brinston resumed his talk-through of the evidence. "It's a bit of a wild card. Although his blood-alcohol level was far from extreme, I can't rule out rapid intake of excessive alcohol that caused vomiting before it could be absorbed in the system, because his stomach was completely empty. However, it could also be related to the head injury. It's not uncommon for someone to vomit after a blow to the head, even with a minor concussion that would have resolved on its own in time. In the hospital, we didn't worry too much, as long as the vomiting was an isolated incident immediately after the head injury and there were no other concomitant neurologic problems. I found minor injury to the brain from the impact and also on the opposite side from where the brain whiplashed inside the skull, but I didn't see any significant swelling or bleeding, although sometimes there can be delayed cerebral edema up to twenty-four hours after injury."

Jones quizzically summed up, "So, no drugs, no ligature marks, yet someone flayed all the skin off his torso."

"Precisely," Brinston said. "You see now why I called you."

Jones addressed his DC, "We really need to get his phone records, as well as all the street camera footage we can grab, Tully. There's got to be something there that will make sense of this. See if you can speed that up, will you?"

Tull nodded and stepped out to make some calls.

"Time of death?" Jones asked.

"I'd place it at three to four in the morning," Brinston answered.

"That fits in our window," Jones affirmed.

The two men looked down at the body in silence, just the latest in a string of times they'd stood together over the remains of what was once a life. "Not much else I can tell you, Detective Chief Inspector. The family's been asking for a quick release of the body. Twenty-four hours, you know." Brinston covered the body with a sheet, peeled off his gloves, and tossed them into a nearby wastebasket.

"Any reason to deny them?" Jones inquired.

The ME shook his head. "I've got everything I need. It's straightforward on my end. It's your end that's tangled, I believe."

"You are not wrong, Dr. Brinston," Jones said heavily. "You are not wrong."

Chapter Ten

"It was a pleasure seeing you again, Mr. Warwick," Vivienne Clark bid farewell as Wilson stepped outside her front door, carefully avoiding Mr. Fiddle's saucer.

"You as well, Mrs. Clark, and thank you again for the lovely lunch," he replied in kind. She'd refused to allow Wilson to take her out to a local restaurant and instead served him three homemade spinach and sweet potato samosas she'd had in her freezer. Served with homemade tamarind chutney, they were delicious, reinforcing the old sentiment that the British had conquered most of the world just so they could finally have some good food.

"I'm so glad you enjoyed it. If you've any more questions just drop by again or send me a message, whichever works best for you."

"Certainly," Wilson replied with a small nod. She closed the thick door, and he returned to the alleyway. The overhead sun filled it with light, casting out the gloom of this morning. Perhaps it was the samosas talking, but Wilson thought it looked rather pretty now.

He'd stayed with Clark for several hours, closely watching everything that she did to placate the ghosts. She'd gone through an entire year's worth of rituals over a four-hour period, which surely went over well with the local ghosts—it was like celebrating all the holidays on the same day. Wilson could unequivocally state that Clark knew what she was doing and she was doing it right—he hadn't seen or heard a single error.

Despite her perfect performance, Wilson had broached the topic of finding her replacement over their late lunch. It had gone better than he thought, as Clark was having similar thoughts, confirming Wilson's general belief that older people didn't have the illusions of possibility that younger people had. There was no confusion about what the future held for them, and "eventually" was coming closer with each passing day.

Clark had suggested a young woman named Joy Ejogo, a single mother who took one of the free art classes at the Great Missenden Community Centre where she volunteered. Wanting to help another artist that she thought would be receptive to the offer, Clark had asked about how recruitment would work. Wilson had gently rebuffed her, stating that wasn't his area of expertise, but he assured her someone would contact her within the week concerning the matter. That seemed to satisfy her.

Wilson mulled over what he knew as he turned upon High Street. If Clark had fulfilled the Salt Mine's end of the treaty—

which Wilson had magically confirmed with the smallest of charms over lunch—that meant the ghosts weren't living up to their end. More worrisome was the recent death—he wasn't ready to jump to "murder" as Clark had, not until he found out what happened. In search of answers, Wilson headed back to the Greysides.

Getting information from official sources would have been ideal, but he wasn't here as David Wilson of Interpol, and Great Missenden was solidly in DCI Jones's territory. The last thing he needed to do was draw attention to himself as Damon Warwick. Luckily, Great Missenden was a true English village, and he could count on the rumor mill to feed him information; his only task then was finding the kernel of truth among the exaggerations, speculations, and flat-out untruths that were inserted with each retelling.

As he expected for a Saturday, the Greysides' pub was packed with locals and visitors alike. Everyone was talking about what had happened this morning. He got a beer, squeezed into a seat at the bar, and listened. In truest small-town tradition, word had spread faster than wildfire. Once everyone had heard a version of what happened, they'd wasted no time getting to the pub to argue that theirs was the truth of the matter. After two beers, Wilson had the gist of the story, at least the parts that everyone agreed upon, and unfortunately, neither the buzz from his charm nor the beers were enough to paper over his worry—a dead man striped of his skin in Abbey Park was definitely murder.

Once the hive mind started repeating itself, Wilson figured he had eked out all the useful information he was going to get from that crowd and decided to get eyes on where the body was found. He was back on High Street, this time going south, past the abbey and into Abbey Park. He didn't know how popular the park normally was on a sunny Saturday afternoon, but it seemed rather busy. He expected families, people with pets, joggers, and young people with nothing better to do, but he got the distinct impression there were also those who were mostly motivated by morbid curiosity. The police tape had been removed, but that didn't stop passersby looking for signs of blood, gore, or death; in Wilson's experience, people were sorrow vultures.

He took the long loop around the park, circumnavigating it to suss out the official paved entrances as well as the unofficial dirt-path ones. He was surprised by how many he found, but considering how little parking there was, people would naturally enter the park wherever they first encountered it. Once Wilson finished his perimeter check, he followed the interior paths, paying particular attention to where the body had been found. All told, it took two hours to walk the whole park, and by the time he got back to his room, he was famished.

Wilson had his fill of local color this afternoon and ordered room service—an amenity the hotel officially offered, but based on the staff's somewhat clumsy execution, Wilson gathered it was uncommon. However, the quality of the food—fish and chips, although at the Greysides, it was called "beer battered haddock with hand-cut chips and mint tartar sauce"—made up for the poor service. In true American spirit, he left a fiver as a tip on the tray.

As nice as the meal was, Wilson's interest was also on the extra salt he'd requested on the side. The new saltcaster that Dr. Weber had created was elegant and good for subterfuge, but it had limited uses, and one of the downsides was its requirement for extremely fine grains of salt. However, Wilson's old tube could use regular-sized table salt. He had a lot of ground to cover—at minimum, the park entrances, as well as the location where the corpse was found. He would need to pick up more salt later when he felt like hunting down a grocer for some fresh fruit, but for now, he should have enough for tonight's objective.

Most ghosts didn't have a magical signature, as they were the remains of a human that had "lost" its body, unlike the insubstantial supernatural creatures that did have signatures. Unfortunately, the general populace sometimes confused them for or lumped them in with ghosts, which made investigations more challenging. There could be some crossover—things that started out as human but over time, changed into something else entirely—think poltergeist or revenants. The last attack on the living, in 1964, was perpetrated by such a vengeful spirit and the ghost community took care of him according to their code—they devoured him into non-existence. So Wilson's first step was to see what was there, magically speaking.

Wilson left his room in haste after his quickly downing his dinner; the sun would be setting in a few hours, and he wanted natural light to avoid drawing attention to his strange behavior. From a distance, using either of his saltcasters could easily be taken for someone smoking, which was a lot less suspicious than roaming the park at night with a flashlight. His plan was to start with a perimeter sweep again, only this time blowing out puffs of salt as he went past each entrance.

It was a warm day, and the slight breeze as late afternoon morphed into early evening made the quick jaunt to the park pleasant. The pre-dusk sky cast soft light at an oblique angle. Wilson would have otherwise enjoyed the walk had his mind not been on other matters. He strolled to the nearest entrance, casually checking his sides and rear for observers, but no one was paying him much mind. He raised his saltcaster to his lips and blew the first dose of magic-detecting salt on the first formal pedestrian entrance to the park. Wilson paused, pretending to tie his shoe, as the salt shifted on the path into a pattern unfamiliar to him. Wilson pulled out his phone and took a picture—*Maybe Chloe and Dot can identify it?* He rose and walked to the second entry, also formal and paved, and again the same saline sigil appeared. *Curiouser and curiouser.*

Wilson mentally ran through the possibilities as he moved to his next position. Two hits of the same sigil at two different paths could be a couple of things: the presence of a magical item on someone who regularly visited the park, the presence of an active magical spell that for unknown reasons entered or exited the park in two different locations, or it could be the trace of a magical creature traveling in the same fashion. He snapped a second picture and was about to send the librarians a message when he thought better of it—best to check the other entrances and the location of the body first. He personally disliked receiving endless text updates from someone who should have just taken more time to put all the information into one message.

Wilson methodically canvassed the park with his saltcasters over the next three hours; the last three stops required the light from his phone, which was still less suspect than a flashlight. Most were a bust, but he saw the same unknown sigil a third time at the old tree where the body was found. It was too much to be a coincidence. He messaged Chloe and Dot with the results of his investigation before heading back to his room at the Greysides for more work.

Chapter Eleven

Aylesbury, Buckinghamshire, UK
29th of June, 10:05 p.m. (GMT+1)

"The Gambia!" DCI Jones shouted out at the television before the buzzer went off.

"Ohh, good answer," his wife cooed. Sarah Jones was curled up against her husband's chest, enjoying his presence after a long day away. He'd returned only a half hour earlier for a warmed-up slice of lasagna, and they were enjoying an hour of decompression before bed. On his long workdays, she recorded the early evening quiz shows they normally watched together so they could enjoy them whenever he returned. "I would have gone with Tunisia," she added after some thought, "but you know how I am with geography."

The question had been "What is the smallest country, by size, in Africa," and they quietly waited until the answers were revealed to find that neither of them would have won.

"Huh, Seychelles. Would have never gotten that one," DCI Jones acquiesced as he rubbed Sarah's arm with his hand.

"It'd be nice to visit, though, Simon," she commented, trying to remember the last time she'd gotten him on a beach that wasn't cold watered.

He kissed her head and said, "Put it on the list." They had a long docket of places that "would be nice to visit someday," but they never seemed to find the right time. Not that either were much bothered by it; they were content in each other's company, regardless of where they were.

As the end-of-show music started, Jones's phone buzzed. He picked it up with his left hand; it was DC Tull. Both of them knew what a late call meant, and Sarah kissed him before rising from the couch and taking their mugs to the sink. "This is Jones," he answered.

"We finally have the camera footage," Tull reported.

"We get a picture?" Jones asked hopefully.

"Yes, but…but I…" Tull stumbled over the words before collecting himself. "You really need to see them yourself, sir."

"Can't you just explain it over the phone?" Jones would have been put out, but DC Tull didn't have a habit of wasting his time.

Silence came over the line, causing Jones to look at his screen to make sure the call hadn't been cut off. Finally Tull spoke, "I don't think I can, sir."

"I'll be there in ten minutes," he said reluctantly.

****

"All right, Tully, what's so difficult to explain?" Jones

grumbled as soon as he was within earshot of DC Tull.

"Over here, sir," Tull called out, waving Jones to his computer. The DC looked tired; Jones couldn't remember if he'd ever seen Tull tired before—the young man was usually full of energy. Jones sat down in the extra chair Tull had set up for him. Tull prefaced the video on his screen, before starting it, "This is from the camera on the intersection of High Street and Martinsend Lane, the road that leads to the train station." The frames started progressing, making a somewhat jumpy viewing.

"How many frames per second do we have here?" Jones inquired.

"It's one of the older traffic cams. I believe it's only six," Tull replied. "We have images from the train station platforms as well. They confirm Mia Davenport's story. But this is where it gets interesting."

Jones grunted and kept watching—modern surveillance cameras typically had at least fifteen frames per second. On the screen, Mr. Farah appeared in the distance, jerkily walking back alone from the train station. When he reached the corner he suddenly turned, running headfirst into a metal pole and then collapsing on the ground. Tull paused and ran the image back and forth, frame by frame, pointing at the screen. "I believe this is where he got both of the head wounds: first impact on the pole and the second—right here—on the concrete."

Jones nodded. "Well, that's one mystery solved. That looks

purely accidental to me."

Tull concurred and started the video again. Farah lay on the ground for nearly thirty seconds before waking, touching his head, and groggily rising, using the pole to steady himself. "Must have been a hard hit, sir. Watch how he has difficulties walking—he has to lean against the building after he gets up."

Jones watched Farah stumble a few times against a building until he passed under a large awning, nearly disappearing from view. Tull paused the video when that happened and opened another window from a different camera. "This is better quality; fifteen frames a second. The direction is facing north along High Street. Mr. Farah is right there."

"I see him Tully," Jones snapped. *What was so unexplainable about this?* "This doesn't tell us how his body got to the park without the skin on his torso."

"Yes, sir. I'm getting to that part," Tull reassured his DCI. "I'll start both videos at the same time."

Jones watched for only a few seconds before a person appeared out of thin air in the middle of the walkway. "What the hell?" the DCI half-whispered.

"I know!" Tull exclaimed. "I don't know where he came from either." The new person was dressed in a robe with the hood covering their head; shortly after their sudden appearance, the victim started vomiting.

"Pause and go back frame by frame, Tully," Jones commanded, crossing his arms and furrowing his brow. "We must have missed something." Tull knew that dogged look on Jones's face all too well.

"I have looked over this footage from every direction possible over and over again. He literally appears out of nowhere. I'll rewind in just a second, but I want you to see this first."

Jones leaned toward the screen as the video started again. Mr. Farah finished vomiting, wiped his left hand against his mouth, and then the robed figure removed his hood, revealing a pale face and a tonsured head. The figure held out his hand, and Mr. Farah grabbed it and stood straight up. Together, they proceeded to walk south.

Jones noted the timestamp on the video. "We need to find that man. That could be the last person to see Mr. Farah alive, or worse, the person that decided to skin him," Jones asserted.

"That's not all, sir," Tull spoke gravely as he advanced the videos side-by-side. Tull was watching Jones as he saw the two figures move down the street and disappear mid-sidewalk.

"You have got to be kidding me!" Jones yelled at the monitor. "They must have turned off somewhere."

"At fifteen frames per second? One of whom just hit his head so hard that he passed out and vomited?" Tull gingerly challenged his DCI's supposition.

Jones wasn't buying it. "There have to be more cameras at some of the intersections on High Street," he posited. "There are the two cameras at Abbey Park."

"I've already look at them, sir. There's no sign of either of them," Tull responded matter-of-factly.

Neither men knew what to say as they stared at the glow of the monitor. "Tully, people just don't disappear," Jones eventually spoke.

"They don't just appear either, sir, but yet…"

Jones shifted in the chair. "Go back to when the hooded figure first appears. Go frame by frame."

Tull did as he was ordered; he knew how many times he had watched it before he'd decided to call Jones. The DCI focused on the screen—there was no one there, but in the very next frame stood the hooded figure, mid-shot. "It only makes it worse, sir," Tull commented from experience.

Chapter Twelve

Great Missenden, Buckinghamshire, UK
30th of June, 12:01 a.m. (GMT+1)

Wilson knew what he needed to do next, but he required a few supplies. He quickly stopped by a store on his way back from Abbey Park and picked up a pack of candles, a lighter, a kilo of salt to replenish his stores, a liter of water, and some snacks for the wait till midnight. When he returned to his turreted room at the Greysides, he moved the furniture to one side and created a large open space within which to operate. He placed six tea light candles in a circle and checked their position before setting them aflame.

Wilson grabbed a quick snack and watered up—once he began, he wouldn't be able to stop until it was done; as soon as he took Weber's dissolvable tablet, the clock was ticking. He turned off the other lights in the room so that it was only illuminated by candlelight. He positioned himself on one side of the circle of candles and waited for the clock to tick one minute past midnight. Only then did Wilson start the séance.

There were several ways for the living to contact the dead, but of those ways, the séance was considered the most respectful. Although it appeared the ghosts were failing to live up to their end of the treaty, he was going to approach the subject with cautious respect. There wasn't anything to be gained by being rude.

As Wilson supplicated into the dim light, he pushed his will outward and moved it in a circular motion, like the swirling waters in a vortex. The rhythmic pull would entice nearby ghosts without forcing them to appear before him. Those who chose to enter the whorl would be able to communicate with him—in a séance, he could only speak with those who wished to be spoken to. Once he established the patter, he slipped in one of Weber's language-translating lozenges and held it under his tongue. It wouldn't be long now.

Wilson closed his eyes and directed a constant stream of will into the eddy he had created. Within a few minutes, the glittering candles flickered and a presence entered the room. "To the spirit who has arrived, my greetings," Wilson spoke in a flat pitch. Strictly speaking, none of the spectacle was needed to speak with a ghost—the candles, the voice modulation, the midnight hour—but it was best to keep up the old ways when encountering an unknown ghost.

Wilson felt the air compress and then a voice emerged out of nothingness, "Who is it that draws our attention?"

More than one ghost, Wilson thought. *Good. That should save time.*

"I am Damon Warwick from the Institute of Tradition, and I am here to speak about the Treaty of Great Missenden," he announced himself.

A voluminous pressure released, as if a depth charge had been dropped into the room. Wilson was physically pushed backward an inch, and he instinctively opened his eyes and drew his will back into his body. He visually swept the area— the candles were still alight, but whoever he had been speaking to had retreated.

Undeterred, Wilson closed his eyes and started whirling his will for a second attempt. This time, a response was nearly immediate. "Mr. Warwick, we are honored to meet you again," a different voice enunciated, seemingly from nowhere. "It would please us greatly to greet you properly, face-to-face."

Wilson opened his eyes to nearly half a dozen translucent figures softly glowing on the other side of his small circle of candles. The two figures in the front were obviously related—their long faces, high foreheads, and aquiline noses spoke to a kinship. Wilson remembered them from the treaty renegotiations: Sir John du Plessis, 7th Earl of Warwick, and his fourth son, Sir Hugh, Lord of Great Missenden. Not only were they the spokesmen for the ghosts ten years ago, they were also the first to sign the original Pacification Treaty in 1917.

"Ah, Sir John, Sir Hugh, a pleasure to meet you again," Wilson hailed them, rising from the ground and giving a small bow. Behind the nobles were two more faces he immediately placed names to: Mrs. Opal Wood, and Miss Clara Felton. There were other faces he recognized, but he couldn't remember their names; it *had* been nearly a decade and there had been a whole group of ghosts involved in the negotiations—the more-modern ghosts translating between the older ghosts and the living. It had been like watching a UN meeting in slow motion; an arduous process, but successful. "Ladies, Gentlemen," he collectively acknowledged the others in the group.

"It has been some time since you were last here, Mr. Warwick," Sir John said cautiously.

"Almost ten years, Sir John, and I feel them. Of course, all of you look exactly the same," Wilson joked to lighten the mood. Although his reasons for contacting them were serious in nature, he didn't want to spook them.

"The benefits of healthy living, Mr. Warwick," Mrs. Wood piped in response; her proper Victorian English danced like the dialogue of a period movie.

"I see you've gained use of our tongue?" Sir Hugh observed with mild surprise. The older ghosts who had just picked up the change nodded with him.

"It is a new magic we've created, Sir Hugh. It is powerful, but lasts only a brief while. Because of that, I'm afraid I need to speak quickly."

"Certainly! Speak your mind," the lord proclaimed.

"We have reason to believe that a little more than a week ago, there was a ghostly attack at the abbey made against one Gemma Green, a woman twenty-four years of age."

A wave of gasps rippled through the ethereal bodies.

"Certainly, sir, you are mistaken!" Mrs. Wood exclaimed.

"Additionally, there was a murdered and skinned gentleman found in Abbey Park yesterday morning, and my initial investigations suggest that there are supernatural forces involved," Wilson reported neutrally, to keep tensions to a minimum. "If the perpetrator in both cases is one of the once-living, aggressions are escalating which neither party of the great peace want."

Shock turned to outrage—a ghost killing one of the living had been unheard of for over a century. "That's impossible!" Sir Hugh vehemently objected over the roiling.

"I come to you to ask for your help in finding the culprit, not to accuse anyone of a crime they did not commit," Wilson raised his volume to be heard over the din. "The Institute of Tradition values our many years of friendship, and does not make this inquiry lightly."

Sir John raised his hand to quiet his council. "We will look into the matter. Rest assured, if a ghost is responsible, we shall find the guilty and deal with the matter directly," he vowed, putting his right arm over his chest. "We are committed to the accord and have dealt with other miscreants that threatened the peace in the past. This shall be no different."

Wilson lowered himself to acknowledge Sir John's words of solidarity. "When you believe you have an answer, or would like to speak again, please just knock my blue shirt off the corner of the dresser." Wilson directed their attention to the article of clothing in question, conveniently placed near the edge of the dresser as a courtesy to the ghosts. The collective spectral heads bobbed in approval.

While ghosts could theoretically manifest on their own accord for a conversation, it took a tremendous amount of energy—an expenditure currently paid for them by Wilson's swirling will. However, knocking over a light object required much less energy and it was something even the weakest of ghosts would be able to do. The appearance of consideration aside, Wilson's ulterior motive was to allow any ghost, regardless of their power or prestige in the community, to contact him privately.

"I only have one more use of this new language-magic, so if you would send one who is conversant in the modern tongue, I would greatly appreciate it," Wilson added. They exchanged more words, assuring each other of their mutual bonds of affection, agreeing to send young Miss Felton to speak with Wilson.

As the ghosts faded out of existence, Wilson released his will. He opened up the liter of water, parched from diplomacy. Conducting a séance was close enough to summoning that he didn't even get a buzz off it. He snuffed out the candles, placing them on the dresser until the liquid wax cooled and solidified. He left the furniture alone for now and flipped on the television instead—surely there would be something entertaining to his jet-lagged brain this late at night. He climbed into bed with the remote and started changing channels.

Chapter Thirteen

Vivienne Clark rose with the sun in summertime, making the most of the clear days and relative warmth. She performed her ablutions, brushed her wavy gray hair, and secured it in a loose braid. Dressed for her morning constitutional—loose slacks, a cotton shirt with a light jacket to cut any dewy chill, and her ochre hiking boots—she took a light breakfast with tea, grabbed her hiking stick, and left through her front door.

Walking the trails was a national obsession that Clark shared with her countrymen. She liked the quiet of the morning, especially during tourist season when visitors abounded and interrupted her commune with nature at any other time of day. She could always tend to her garden if the outdoors called to her later on in the day.

Clark had much on her mind this morning. Mr. Warwick's visit was certainly a surprise, although not unpleasant. She knew there was a whole other realm of things she didn't understand, but took pride in playing her part. Retirement wasn't something she had considered, since her job had afforded her decades of financial security with minimal inconvenience. When the kids were young, the stability of home and routine was ideal, and her husband George, rest his soul, was never one for long trips to exotic locales—her having to be back in time to perform the weekly rituals was rarely a hardship. When George passed, it gave her time purpose while she worked out how to be alone after years of being a half of something.

The Institute of Tradition had been good to her and provided for her through the ups and downs of life, but she didn't really need stability anymore. Her kids had grown and flown the nest, her art had gone as far as it was going to go, and the routine was just that. Perhaps it was time to pass the opportunity to another, someone who needed the safety of routine and security instead of someone who had just grown accustomed to it.

But Clark had too much respect for her work and the Institute to just retire. She had to find a suitable replacement, maybe stay long enough to train her. Clark wasn't opposed to passing the baton to a man, but in her experience, women were more reliable when it came to keeping the old ways. She suspected that given enough time, a man would want to improve upon it, but that wasn't the point of ritual.

When Joy Ejogo first entered Clark's beginner watercolor class at the Great Missenden Community Centre, she drew the old woman's attention. There was something unique in her quiet, thoughtful manner and in her piercing and perceptive eyes that saw the lines behind the form and depths in color. Clark learned of Ejogo's five-year-old, when she missed a few classes last winter when he was sick with a bad cold that went into his chest. Ejogo returned to class despite her absences, which Clark interpreted as a sign of her commitment to intangible things like art.

When Mr. Warwick had showed up at her front door and brought up the idea of her replacement, something sparked inside of her. Clark's chest swelled with the new breath of possibility. She wasn't religious per se, but she always believed that the universe gave you what you needed, even if it wasn't necessarily what you asked for.

Clark came to a fork in the path and took the loop back into town. It was Sunday, and she had things to do. If there was one thing Clark understood, it was ritual. She stopped by the florist's and picked up her standing weekly arrangements: one red and blue asters, and the other white and pink carnations. She walked to the graveyard and found her husband of forty-five years and her daughter, who had lived less than a month. She cleared last week's flowers and the incidental debris that had blown over their graves before depositing the fresh bouquets.

She circled back to the bakery and picked up something more substantial for an early lunch and bought a copy of the Sunday paper before returning home. The first thing she did when she arrived home was unhooked the laces of her boots and trading them in for house shoes. Next, she put the kettle on for tea and warmed up her spinach and cheese quiche, readying a pretty plate for her Sunday treat—you eat with your eyes first.

Once everything was set, she took a seat at her breakfast table with a view of her garden and laid out the paper. Clark got as far as two bites of her quiche before she put her fork down, staring at the headline below the fold: Murder in Great Missenden. She ran her fingertips along the pixilated color photo of Mo Farah, recognizing him from the tour group. She skimmed the article, which was light on details as "there is an ongoing investigation" and "the police are treating this as a suspicious death." She sat, stunned, as her quiche grew cold. According to the paper, he was found dead in Abbey Park not five hours after taking her tour. A shiver ran down her spine.

*****

"Ugh," Evelyn huffed at the burgundy merino swatch in her hands. "How did I get off pattern? I used markers and kept track of my rows…" She left her work on the table and rose to get another slice of lemon drizzle cake to go with her cup of tea. The circle of women kept their heads and their snickers down.

"I'm sure it's nothing that can't be mended," Bobby looked up and spoke soothingly as her needles clicked together at a rapid pace. As she finished her row and her counter ticked over by one, she put her yoke down and moved over to Evelyn's seat.

"Let's see what can be done."

Bobby Knolls was the owner of Shear Panic, a shop dedicated to textile arts of all varieties. Originally her mother's shop, Bobby had taken it over when she'd passed twenty years ago, and steered it into the twenty-first century. Being her mother's daughter, she had spent a lifetime sewing, stitching, embroidering, knitting, and crocheting, but when the time had come to apply her business acumen from her day job to her crafting, Bobby's fate was sealed and Shear Panic was born.

Bobby had ridden the waves of whim and fancy, playing up whatever was considered hot or retro-chic in the moment. Social media was a beautiful thing; as soon as an actress talked about how she knits on set between scenes or was photographed wearing something she made, a swath of women—many of whom were younger than her standard clientele—came into her shop looking for supplies, patterns, and classes.

Evelyn was a recent addition to the shop's Sunday afternoon Stitch and Bitch—a time for women to bring whatever project they were working on and enjoy each other's company. In reality, it was really an excuse to eat cake, drink tea—sometimes something stronger—and gossip. Evelyn was a nurse at the hospital who had recently decided that she needed something that was "just for her," and found her way to Shear Panic. She was in her late thirties and new to knitting, and the old guard had taken her in and closed ranks.

Bobby held the swatch in the light and found the irregularity.

"See here? You repeated a row and knitted these two stitches together. That's why you don't have enough stitches and your stockinette stitch is off."

Evelyn looked over Bobby's shoulder at the nub that was supposed to eventually be a scarf. "So how to do I fix it?"

"Take it off the needle, rip out the rows until you get back to the pattern, and slip the stitches back on the needle," Carol chimed in.

"Rip out rows?!" Evelyn asked in disbelief.

"Don't worry. We have all been there and had to do it. It's the only way to save the work you've already done," Patty reassured her.

"Can you do it for me?" Evelyn nervously asked Bobby.

"I can if you want me to, but it's better if you learn how to do it," Bobby replied. "Patty's right—it happens more often than any of us would like to admit." The circle of heads bobbed in agreement.

The bell on the front door chimed as Vivienne Clark entered. "Hello, ladies. I brought zucchini bread." They made room at the table as Clark left the sweets on the non-work table. She sidled her way between Carol and Patty and pulled out her embroidery. Clark was in French knot hell, but there was nothing to be done about it—it was the only way to get the texture and effect of the flower blooms.

Evelyn was pulling her stitches out at a snail's pace under Bobby's watchful eye, while the others caught up on the news great and small. The body in Abbey Park was foremost in everyone's mind, and they shared what they had heard with each other. There was a mix of disbelief and awe when Clark told them the victim had been on her evening ghost tour the night he died.

A hush came over the table when the front door bell chimed again. They waited for a familiar female voice to greet them, but instead heard a man speak, "Excuse me? Is anyone inside?"

Bobby patted Evelyn's shoulder and emerged from the back room reserved for classes and events. She found the strapping figure of DC Tull at the door of her shop. "Hello. Can I help you?"

Tull pulled out his identification. "Hello, I'm Detective Constable Tull. I'm investigating the murder that happened in the area last night, and I saw you have a camera covering the front of your shop."

"Yes, my son insisted we have video of the front, as some of our classes and events occur at night," Bobby answered him after looking at his badge.

"I see. Do you have a record of the video from two nights ago?" Tull inquired hopefully.

"I think so. I have to change out a new CD every week, so I would imagine it's recording. My son set it up for me," Bobby replied.

Tull kept his composure. *What video system still uses CDs?* "If you would be so kind as give us access to the video, it could help with the investigation."

Bobby clapped and rubbed her hand together. "Certainly, officer. Right this way." She led DC Tull through the back room where a table of four women sat quietly working on sewing and yarn things. Bobby disappeared into a small room that doubled as storage and her office. It was entirely too small for both of them to stand inside comfortably, so Tull waited outside the doorway, acutely aware of the collective weight of sideways glances and unspoken curiosity coming from the circle of women, even though their hands were in motion and their eyes fixed to their crafts. He felt a bit like shrimp cocktail at a buffet.

Eventually, Bobby came out of the small back office and produced a CD. Tull slipped it into an evidence bag and thanked her for her time. The room stayed quiet until they heard the bell mark Tull's exit.

"He was handsome," Carol noted in Evelyn's general direction—the divorce was finalized three months ago. Evelyn said nothing, starting her next row, making sure her stockinette stitch was right.

"What's on the CD?" Patty quizzed Bobby.

"The video from the camera out front. You know, the one Mark insisted I put up so that we wouldn't be ravished during our evening classes," she answered.

"And they think there may be something on it about the young man that was murdered?" Clark wondered aloud.

"Well, there's only one way to find out," Bobby quipped back and pulled up her phone. She tapped away at the screen while she spoke, "My grandson gave me a lecture about how I should back everything up on the cloud, so eventually, I let him come by and hook everything up. We should be able to see the video from the camera, I just have to download it from my account."

Everyone found a good place to stop and huddled around Bobby's phone—it beat knitting and French knots.

Chapter Fourteen

Barking, London, UK
30th of June, 12:45 p.m. (GMT+1)

Wilson's blue Vauxhall Corsa buzzed south along the A406; he had a one o'clock appointment with Gemma Green, and a traffic accident had put him behind his normally well-padded arrival time. The compact car weaved in and out of traffic in hopes of regaining a few extra minutes from the time he lost due to rubbernecking drivers.

His day had started slow. After a busy day yesterday, Wilson had every intention of enjoying a lazy Sunday morning lie in. His corner room was spared direct morning sunlight, and he had the foresight to pull down the window shades before turning in for the night.

Consequently, his phone had roused him from his sleep with a message from the Salt Mine, only just beating the church bells ringing for service. He had hoped it was word from Chloe and Dot on the signature, but alas, it was additional background information for his current Warwick alias that the Mine had spun to Green's manager, Alistair Thumbold.

Thumbold and Green had been told Warwick was a columnist from the American branch of the Institute of

Tradition, and that his interest in her story was driven by the popularity of *A Bump in the Night* stateside. It had taken two days of negotiations, but the thousand-pound payment they'd offered eventually eased any concerns the two Brits may have had about his authenticity.

It wasn't the first time his Institute of Tradition alias had proved useful. The Institute was a worldwide organization with at least one branch on every continent. Its stated mission was documenting and preserving the local traditions of various peoples and places within their respective geographic domains. Collectively, they produced an English-language quarterly named *The Way Things Were*. Every issue had at least one story from each continent, and existed solely to provide cover for agents who needed a quick reason to start asking questions.

After fully waking, Wilson had spent what remained of the morning eating a late breakfast and going back over the collection of media coverage the Mine had gathered for him. The first thing he noticed was the lack of face-to-face interviews on television or the internet—either Gemma Green wasn't that famous, or the story wasn't sensational enough for mass consumption.

Reading through the different tabloids, Wilson had a basic understanding of the event as retold by the actress. Green had returned to her room after a long night shoot, changed, and gotten into bed. Just as she was falling asleep, the covers were pulled over her head and she was beaten, suffering dozens of blows in quick succession that left dark bruises across her back and torso. The covers then flew off her bed, and she felt like she was being attacked by some type of sharp instrument. The images were shocking—as tabloid pictures tend to be. Her entire back was covered with bruises, with scratch marks all over her body, particularly around her neck and waist. Whatever was attacking Green was interrupted by one of the *A Bump in the Night's* crew, who had knocked down her door once he heard her screaming. Afterward, Green had been taken to the Chiltern Hospital for treatment.

Wilson mulled the information over in his head as he pulled off the A406 via the Barking exit—the UK had the best place names in the world—and followed his phone's GPS to his destination with five minutes to spare. He hated being late, and thanked his luck for the lone open parking space on the one-way lane of row houses. He quickly reminded himself of who he was supposed to be before exiting the vehicle and hustling to Green's door.

His solid knock was opened almost immediately, which suggested to Wilson that his approach had been observed. On the other side was a remarkably beautiful young woman who Wilson recognized as Gemma Green from his files. When her manager had called her this morning, Gemma had been put out by the short notice, but she was a professional. *A Sunday afternoon interview?* As she did her makeup and dressed with deliberate care, she considered the unusualness of the request. She had selected something casual that brought attention to her assets, and chose subtle makeup that highlighted her natural beauty. "Mr. Warwick?" she asked, full well knowing the answer.

Wilson extended his hand. "Yes. Please call me Damon. So nice to meet you, Ms. Green." She quickly accepted it and Wilson noted that her hand was smooth and soft, perhaps even a bit greasy, as if she'd just moisturized and had yet to absorb the entire product. Despite the transferred lingering scent of lilac honeysuckle, Wilson fought the urge to wipe his hand on his pants after they broke contact.

"Call me Gemma," she greeted him and motioned for him to enter. Her house had that recently cleaned look—roughshod attempts at tidying so the piles of junk looked more like eclectic collections, and a slapdash dusting done in a hurry with lines showing how things had been dusted around instead of removed and dusted under. The decor had a decidedly inspirational theme. There were small little hangings throughout the front entrance and sitting room: *live, laugh, love* and *live out loud.* His favorite tromp through banality hung on a wooden frame over the brick fireplace: *Life is not measured by the breaths you take, but by the moments that take your breath away.*

Wilson declined the inevitable offer of tea and after a few pleasantries, he got to the point, "Gemma, the Institute has a real interest in any contact with the supernatural, and we think your experience could be very enlightening for our readers. I've read what others reporters have written, but I would really like to hear it in your own words."

Green softened at his tone; the media had treated her

badly about the whole thing, accusing her of lying or attention seeking. It was refreshing to have someone simply believe her and want to listen to her; he hadn't even ogled her on the sly once—and she knew when she was being checked out. "Well, it was just a normal night, you know? You're familiar with the show, so you know how they split up into groups and investigate various areas, right? Nothing much happened while we wandered about, and I eventually went to bed. That's where it happened.

"It all happened so fast. I was nearly asleep when the covers were slammed over my head and I was held down and beaten. It was so scary!" Her face screwed up, but she quickly turned away from Wilson and stood up, pulling off her top without a hint of self-consciousness. The smooth skin of her back was a mottled mess of bruises from deep purples to sallow yellows. The scratches, while numerous, were mostly superficial—more in line with a very angry house cat than those of a larger animal—but there were a few deeper ones.

"Jesus, that's bad!" Wilson exaggerated for her benefit.

"I know, right?" She looked over her shoulder. "Do you want to take some pictures?"

There was little doubt in Wilson's mind that Ms. Green was performing for him, but it was difficult to discern just how much of this display was part of her processing recent events. He was hardly impressed by the damage, given the collection of scars he bore, but he decided to give her the benefit of the doubt—people dealt with trauma in different ways.

Wilson pulled out his phone and started snapping photos, taking full-body shots as well as close ups. Once she heard his phone's camera shutter, Gemma turned around so he could capture the injuries on her sides and front.

Wilson noticed the circumferential pattern around her midsection. "I thought you were lying in bed…how did you get scratches all around your waist?"

"I have no idea," Green replied. "Everything happened in the blink of an eye, like less than a minute, and it was dark—just the light from under the door and the clock." She marveled at how he was definitely not looking at her breasts.

Wilson nodded and continued snapping photos, especially those circumscribing her neck and deltoids, which appeared worse than those on her torso, "And all the way around the shoulders?"

Green raised her arms. "Even in my armpits. You have any idea how painful that is?"

"I can only imagine," he responded. "Did the cops take a statement from you?"

"They did, but they didn't believe me," she decried petulantly. "They think this was all faked for publicity for the show."

"That's ridiculous!" Wilson feigned indignation. "The amount of time it would have taken you to stage this, the amount of pain you would have to have gone through….it doesn't make sense."

"Precisely!"

After a few final snaps, Wilson said, "I think I have all the photos I need."

Green threw her shirt on with a quick motion, perplexed at this strange little man in her living room. "You know, the weirdest part was that there was no blood on the sheets. I still don't understand how that happened. You saw all those scratches; they look a lot better now, but I was a bloody mess that night. That was the reason they took me to the hospital—I was bleeding everywhere. How could none of it have gotten on the bed?"

Wilson didn't have an adequate response to the question and gave a baffled shrug. He understood why the police questioned the veracity of her story—the physical evidence didn't match her account, none of the scratches were deep enough to require stitches, and despite the thorough beating on her torso, there was no damage to her face—but he saw little to be gained in pointing that out to the actress.

Instead, he steered the interview forward, gathering the bits of information he would need to streamline his investigation and to sell his cover. "So, Gemma, it's obvious you were attacked by some supernatural force. We at the Institute of Tradition would love to tell your story, but we'll need a few more details about yourself to help paint the full picture for our readers."

****

The rest of the interview took about two hours. By the

end, he knew everything he'd ever wanted to know about Ms. Gemma Green, but most importantly, he knew her room number at the Great Missenden Abbey the night of the attack. He was looking up the phone number for the abbey when his phone rang; the call was identified as Vivienne Clark. "This is Damon Warwick," he answered.

"Damon, I hate to bother you, but I think I have something you'd like to see," she spoke warily.

"Okay," Wilson replied. "I'm in London right now, but I can be at your place in about an hour."

"I'm not at home," she qualified. "I'm in a fabric store called Shear Panic, on High Street. A friend of mine runs the store, and her security cameras caught something strange about the murder." She lowered her voice to almost a whisper, "The police were just here."

"Perfect! I'll be there in an hour," Wilson said enthusiastically. They ended the conversation, and he called Great Missenden Abbey to book a room for the night. A quick search found the store's address, which he entered into the phone's GPS before starting up the Vauxhall. Wilson darted his blue rental westward through light traffic, keeping his driving just on the edges of legal, all the while his mind raced.

He wished he could work with local law enforcement on the murder, but he was already here as Damon Warwick of the Institute, and DCI Jones knew him as David Wilson of Interpol. Having the Salt Mine fabricate a story that would be consistent with both would not be impossible, if absolutely necessary, but he'd rather not draw attention to himself. Still, the prospect of getting his hands on some hard evidence was a step forward.

Wilson found the store with ease, but parking on High Street, even on a Sunday, was more challenging. He parked a few blocks away and enjoyed the short stroll on another beautiful summer's day, soaking in the sun before entering Shear Panic. A high-pitched ding of an electronic doorbell sounded on his entry, and Wilson took in his surroundings.

Every surface was covered with textiles of one sort or another. One whole wall was covered in cubbies packed with a rainbow of yarn, from the finest fingering, past worsted weight, and straight into the thick chunky stuff. There were clusters of upright bolts of cloth organized by color, patterns, and designers. Huge rollers of batting and extra-wide backing loaded horizontally on solid steel racks stood to one side. Every surface had a rack or cabinet displaying buttons, notions, needles, gauges, and cutters. Hung from the ceiling were top quilts from the traditional to the whimsical. Wilson was acutely aware he was in another world not his own, and stood a few feet within the threshold. "Hello?" he called out to the empty room.

"We're back here, Damon!" Clark responded and her voice carried through a small hallway that led out of the commercial area of the store. Wilson followed the sound of her voice and suddenly found himself confronted by a table of women carefully working on various projects.

"Ladies," he greeted them with a nod to the room. His acknowledgement was silently noted by the women of the Stitch and Bitch, and held in stark comparison to DC Tull's manners earlier in the day. Clark was sitting at the back table along with a dark-haired woman; unlike the other ladies, neither of them were working on a craft. They both rose as he entered, and Clark waved him to follow her even further back.

"This is Bobby Knolls; she owns the shop," Clark introduced her friend.

"Nice to meet you, Ms. Knolls," he addressed her with a handshake.

"You as well, Mr....?"

"Warwick," he answered.

"Mr. Warwick...Vivienne took one look at the video and said you'd be interested," Bobby summed up her understanding. It had been a jarring Sunday, all things considered.

"I have no doubt that's the case," Wilson replied as he followed her into a truly tiny room. He had to squeeze behind her as she sat down in a folding chair in front of a security console. Clark stood in the doorway, where she had a good view of the both the screen and his face.

"This is from the exterior camera on the shop," Knolls explained as she pressed play. Wilson hunched over her shoulder and oriented the camera angle—set just under cover of the exterior awning facing south—and carefully watched the short video. It was grainy and a bit jumpy, but everything was easily discernable.

He grunted in interest when the monk appeared, and Clark caught the briefest predatory mien pass over his face before it was replaced by confusion at the disappearance of the two figures after they'd traveled a few steps south.

"Could you play that again?" he requested intently.

Knolls complied. "I'd never believed Vivienne's stories—sorry Vivienne—but this makes a believer out of me. That's the Black Monk all right, and in front of my store!"

Wilson ignored her chatter. "Would you play it one more time, please?" He leaned in close, carefully comparing the shadows cast by the street lamp on the corner to confirm what he thought he'd seen. Both figures in the video had shadows. That meant that whatever the figure was, he knew it wasn't a ghost—ghosts were incapable of casting shadows.

"This is the man who was found murdered?" he asked, confirming what he'd been told.

"Yes," Clark responded. "I had given him a Greater Missenden ghost tour earlier in the evening."

Wilson straightened. "Is it possible I could have a copy of this, Ms. Knolls?"

Wilson saw the ladies exchange quick glances before the shop owner spoke, "Of course. I downloaded this from the cloud, so if you'd just give me your e-mail address, I'll mail it to you."

Wilson extricated himself from the close quarters to retrieve one of his business cards. As Knolls attached the file to the e-mail, he quietly pulled Clark aside and spoke in a hushed tone, "I'd like to speak privately with you some time soon."

"I was just about to leave, so if you want, you could escort me home," she suggested.

"That sounds good," he replied. Knolls piped up, informing him that the message had been sent. Wilson quickly checked his phone to make sure he'd received it, and thanked her for everything she'd done. "This is the most remarkable thing I've ever seen," he lied. "I'm going to have to keep quiet on it for a while, however, as the police are interested in it. But rest assured, it will see publication. The study of ghosts is of great scientific importance."

Knolls and the other ladies in attendance were adequately impressed by Wilson's proclamation, although they would not compare observations until after he and Clark left the shop. Clark gathered her things and made her goodbyes. Wilson waited and held the door open for her. Once they were outside Shear Panic, Clark wagered a guess, "Something's wrong, isn't it?"

Wilson nodded. "I don't know what we saw, but it definitely wasn't a ghost. Can you tell me about the tour you gave the night of the murder?"

Clark looked at a loss. "What do you want to know?"

"Where did you start? What did you talk about? Which path did you walk?" Wilson nudged her.

Clark paused to collect her thoughts before she resumed walking; Wilson waited until she was ready, and let her set their pace. "It's all variations on the same theme. We started at the

Greysides, and I told them about the gravestones lining the building. We walked down High Street, and I went through séances and all the usual suspects—Clara Felton, Johnathan Blake, and the Livingstones. I remember they were really interested in ghosts, and the four of them had just formed a group, Chiltern something or other. Then we went to the abbey, and I always use that dark spooky stretch to talk about the Black Monk. We made a couple of stops around the outside of the abbey and went through the park before circling back to the Greysides."

Wilson mentally mapped the tour's route. "Do you remember which entrance and exit you used through the park?"

Clark thought it an odd question, but answered nonetheless. "We entered on the back abutting the abbey and exited out the main entrance. I like to keep to the paved paths at night—fewer turned ankles."

"Did you pass the old tree where they found the dead body?" Wilson posed a question as they paused at a light, waiting for the crosswalk light.

Clark shook her head back and forth. "No, I don't go near the river on night tours. It's muddy, and its location is somewhat unpredictable year-to-year." Wilson puzzled—only one point on Clark's path through the park bore the unknown magical signature, so it was unlikely that whatever it was followed them throughout the tour.

"Did anything unusual happen on the tour?" Wilson fished. "Did you or one of your guests feeling something, hear something, sense something?"

Clark shrugged as they turned down the alleyway leading to her house. "I can't say anything out of the ordinary happened that evening." Even though it had only been two days, she had given that tour so many times, things blurred together and nothing stood out in her mind. "I'm sorry I couldn't be more helpful."

Wilson quickly reassured her, "You've already been helpful. With your call, I now know it is not a ghost."

Clark perked up. "Yes, I suppose that's something," she said with a smile. After a quiet moment, they reached her door and said their goodbyes. "If there's anything I can do, just let me know," she offered.

"There is one thing you could do. Do you have an old wire clothes hanger? Preferably two?"

Chapter Fifteen

Great Missenden, Buckinghamshire, UK
30th of June, 5:15 p.m. (GMT+1)

Wilson had been unable to book the room Green had stayed in, but he was nonplussed. Entry into a hotel room shouldn't prove too difficult, especially since he arrived early and there were only a few cars outside. Either most of the guests had yet to arrive or they were still enjoying their Sunday out.

Under the guise of looking for his room, Wilson did a quick reconnaissance of the hall, getting a feel for the layout and checking for cameras. There was one close to the room he needed to enter, but the path was otherwise clear. Once he assessed his target, Wilson entered his room and put his mostly empty overnight bag on the bed. He had kept his room at the Greysides—his blue shirt still on the dresser's edge, should the ghosts of Missenden need to talk to him—and hung the "Do Not Disturb" sign before he left. Not only would it have been profoundly odd to come to a hotel with no luggage, but he needed somewhere to stash the wire clothes hanger he'd gotten from Clark and a cheap pair of shoelaces he bought after walking her home.

The rooms at Great Missenden Abbey had recently been

renovated; the public professed a love for "experiencing history" but seemed more pleased when it came with modern amenities. Wilson appreciated the quality of the updates, particularly the unusually thick carpet and foam mattress, but he missed the panache of the turret in his room at the Greysides—this room felt a little sterile.

Wilson unwound one of the wire hangers and worked out the kinks against a chair leg. Once the metal was mostly straight, he bent the hook over and created a loop at one end. On the opposite end, he bent the last six inches into a ninety-degree angle. He spun it around to test its balance and found it acceptable. Using his own room door as a guide, he tied two shoelaces together to form a long enough pull to reach the door handle and secured one end to the loop in the metal. From start to finish, the whole process had taken less than five minutes, but he had a functional under-door tool.

Wilson tucked his improvised under-door tool into his jacket and walked down the hall with his vape pen. Once he was within ten meters of the camera, he turned on the signal jammer and directed it toward the camera, securing it on the wall with duct tape above eye level. He quickly removed the tool and slid it under the door of room twenty-two, keeping a hold on the six-inch handle and the end of the shoelace. Once it was fully advanced, he rotated it using the handle until he felt it catch the lever of the interior door handle. Wilson coordinated his hands and head: pulling on the shoelace and bending the wire to pull the interior latch down from the inside, while applying pressure on the door's exterior with his forehead to push it open the moment the latch gave. It was not unlike patting your head, rubbing your belly, and chewing bubblegum.

Once the door swung open, he entered the room and locked the deadbolt behind him—if the registered guest tried to enter and found it locked, he or she would return to the front desk to complain, and Wilson could make his exit then. *If people knew how vulnerable hotel rooms were, they'd never travel,* he thought with a self-satisfied smile as he surveilled the messy room before him.

Wilson quickly threw the rumpled covers over the bed to even out the surface and blew salt on the top duvet. It had been more than a week since Green was attacked; if there was a signature, it would be weak and rather indistinct, but he should still be able to identify it. It didn't take long before the salt danced across the damask cover and formed a crisp signature—the same as his previous casts in the park. A frown crossed Wilson's face. As pleased as he was to confirm that the same entity who murdered Farah also attacked Green, and that the being wasn't a ghost, the strength of the signature was concerning. A strong sign in the salt this late after the incident meant a powerful source.

Wilson snapped another picture on his phone before throwing the covers off the bed. The salt scattered onto the thick carpet where it disappeared into the pile. He rumpled the sheets and staged them as he'd found them. He gathered his kit under his jacket and left the room after checking through the peephole that the hall was empty. A quick motion ripped his vape pen off the wall, and in a second he was nonchalantly walking down the hallway as if nothing had happened. He returned to his room, hid the under-door tool beneath the center of the mattress, and left the abbey.

He now had four matching signatures, one of which demonstrated significant strength. He walked down High Street and discreetly cast salt from his vape pen outside the doors of Shear Panic. *Make that five*, Wilson thought as he moved past the storefront on his way back to the Greysides. He knew he faced a single opponent—a powerful one, and one about which he knew very little.

His room at the Greysides was much the same as he left it; the furniture was still pushed aside for possible future séances and his blue shirt remained perched on the dresser. He pulled out his phone and sent the picture from Green's room to the Salt Mine with a message: *GG and MF attacked by same. NOT ghost. Please advise on sig.*

He checked his Girard-Perregaux, which showed him the time across the globe; he didn't like the fact that Chloe and Dot hadn't gotten back to him yet. With their eidetic memory, it never took them long to answer him on something simple, like identifying a magical signature that was unknown to him.

His stomach rumbled for food, and Wilson decided to venture down to the pub for an early dinner and a pint while he waited.

The text message he received from the Mine a little over an hour later did little to relieve his apprehension: *Sig unknown. Fae? OLD.* It had to be very rare if Chloe and Dot couldn't identify it or dig it up in the library. Wilson put away his phone and looked around the pub, which had slowly filled as the evening wore on. *It had to be fae*, he sighed and ordered another pint before heading back to the abbey for the night.

Chapter Sixteen

Great Missenden, Buckinghamshire, UK
1st of July, 11:45 a.m. (GMT+1)

Wilson had spent most of the morning gathering the materials he would need for the summoning. Ironically, the hardest to find was actual chalk from England. It was one of the many quirks about the fae—summoning circles would only work if they were drawn with the chalk of their native land. This was one instance where modern globalization was a bane to practitioners of the arts, because most of the materials called chalk aren't actually chalk. Wilson needed real calcium carbonate, not the calcium sulfate of sidewalk chalk, nor the magnesium carbonate or titanium dioxide of the two most common sports' chalks. Eventually, he had given up on finding a place that sold real chalk and instead drove to one of the modern chalk figures that dotted the hillsides. Using his Vauxhall's tire iron, he had mined his own.

Clark had willingly offered him use of her shed for the summoning, provided he let her watch—she had lived long enough to sense an opportunity. Wilson hadn't been pleased with the stipulation, but there wasn't anywhere else as secure and he could not be interrupted during the summoning.

Reluctantly, he had agreed, but with his own set of rules—she would say nothing and do nothing during his preparations and the summoning itself, and whatever happened would stay between them. Once she had sworn agreement to his terms, he began in earnest.

Wilson took his purloined English chalk and laid down the circles on Clark's slate-covered dais, meticulously making sure each point made contact. As a general rule, he disliked summoning the fae—give him a malignant demon any day—so he decided to make his inquiries among the weakest of them: the rat riders. Rat riders were small faeries, no greater than the size of his pinky, and as their name implied, they rode rats. They were also terrible gossips and easy to attract and appease—a chunk of cheddar placed in the center of the small summoning circle would suffice.

He looked to the side and found Clark sitting against the wall, watching intently. They exchanged nods, and Wilson kneeled on a cushion and positioned the unguents on either side of him, careful that nothing touched the circle. He removed his shirt, and Clark concluded that Damon Warwick was more than he appeared to be. She would have never guessed how muscular he was under his clothing—he was a small man that didn't go out of his way to draw attention to his physique. Then there were the scars of past injuries scattered over his torso and arms, but the line of knotted flesh on his left side took the cake. Whoever Damon Warwick was, clearly he had been in the thick of it.

Wilson started chanting, and his melodic voice filled the shed. Faeries were a musical folk, and song was needed to call them from their realm through the Magh Meall, and then into the mortal realm. He smeared a long diagonal mark of rowanberry and thyme paste across his chest after the third repetition and again after the fourth, forming an X. After the fifth and final verse, he encircled the X in paste and amassed his will. He extruded his power around the summoning circle until it fully encompassed; only then did he bear down, pressurizing the circle until it felt like it was under a mile of water.

Clark felt a change in the air and her clinched hands stiffened, like how all her friends described arthritis. Wilson pressed harder and harder until a palpable pop emanated from the circumference of the circle and the barrier fell. Clark stifled her gasp when a tiny humanoid with butterfly wings fluttered within the circle, appearing out of thin air.

"Welcome to the world of the mortals, grand fae," Wilson intoned, as if the miniscule creature was the grandest potentate of its realm.

The creature ignored him and started on the hunk of cheddar. Wilson waited as it ate—it would address him when the offering was fully accepted. It didn't take long for the winged being to finish the cheese, despite the fact it was at least four times its size. Sated, it turned its tiny multifaceted eyes toward the one who'd called it.

"Why have you summoned me, mortal?" Its voice was high in the human register and luxuriously soft. Its unearthly beauty nearly brought tears to Clark, who imagined that was what angels sounded like if they were real.

"I seek information on the state of your domain; how goes it in the lands across the Magh Meall?"

The faerie flew up, laboriously circling within the bounds of its summoning circle—rat riders could fly, but not very well nor for very long—until it was at eye level with the kneeling Wilson.

"Are you a good druid or a bad druid?" it intoned.

"That depends on what you mean by good or bad," Wilson replied guardedly.

The fae let loose a lyric laugh and declared, "You are a cautious druid."

"That I am," Wilson affirmed.

"But are you good or evil?" it reiterated persistently.

"I like to think I'm good, but there are those who would think otherwise," he responded simply.

"And would they be wrong?" the tiny creature pressed, faceted eyes reflecting light from all directions.

After a long pause, Wilson acquiesced, "They would not be wrong." This was why he hated dealing with the fae. The truth—as well as the magician could understand it—was the only safe way of communicating with them. If words were hedged or meanings blended, they would find a way to twist it. Ambiguity and ambivalence were where fae thrived, and a lack of self-awareness was the great danger when dealing with them. Wilson much preferred devils and demons; even though they employed similar tactics of semantic manipulation, it was possible for a magician to get somewhere with them without telling them a lot, much less the truth.

"And you are strong?" the rat rider quizzed him.

Wilson wondered where it was going with these questions. Rat riders tended to be flighty, and its persistence was unusual. Wilson was acutely aware he had an audience—he preferred Clark know as little about him as possible, so he answered obliquely, "What are you asking?"

Wilson didn't know one could roll compound eyes, but the rat rider managed. "Are you strong?" it repeated itself. "When you test yourself against others of your kind, do you triumph?"

"I have been tested and I'm still alive," Wilson commented flatly.

The tiny creature struggled to say at eye level as it waited for a longer answer that it was never going to receive. Eventually, it surrendered to gravity and landed gracefully within the chalk circle. It struggled to catch its breath before asking, "Who's the other mortal?"

"No one of importance to our affair," Wilson emphatically stated.

The rat rider circumvented Wilson's assertion and spoke to Clark, "Mr. Fiddles thinks highly of you, bringer of cream."

It bowed deeply, leveling its gossamer wings parallel with the ground.

Wilson looked sidelong at Clark and gave a shake of his head, reinforcing that she shouldn't say anything—he'd prefer she didn't place herself in danger. Clark remained quiet—something in his eyes made the hairs stand on the back of her neck.

Wilson redirected the faerie, "As I said earlier, I'm interested in knowing the recent affairs of the land across the Magh Meall."

"And I am interested in telling you, but fear that were I to do such, I would put myself in danger," it spoke without reserve.

"I do not wish to put you in danger," Wilson quickly responded. *What could cause a gossip to hold its tongue?* "But I, too, am concerned about danger. Mortals under my care have perished at the hands of a fae."

The tiny fae considered Wilson's statement. "You are like the flies of May, are you not? Why worry that the inevitable comes one of your eye blink's sooner?"

"It is the rarity that makes it precious," Wilson explained, knowing it wouldn't understand, "and I have sworn a promise."

"Ah, a promise is another matter," the creature agreed. "Promises are real." It sat down on its tiny haunches, holding its head in its hands, elbows on knees. It hummed a tuneless drone briefly to itself before growing silent. "It is decided then," it said with some finality.

Wilson raised his eyebrows. "What's decided?"

"You need to come with me to the Magh Meall," it responded resolutely.

He fought the urge to smirk at the diminutive faerie. "And why would I do that?"

"You want to know the state of the land of the fae, so that means you know that change has come, which means that you have power—perhaps power enough to walk the Magh Meall and learn of the changes where the change changed?"

Wilson was getting lost in the rat rider's language. "You're saying that I will learn what I want to know if I follow you to the Magh Meall?"

The little creature stood and bobbed its head.

"I could always force you to tell me," Wilson threatened.

"And if you did so I would tell you…but then, by knowing, you would know you knew not and would never know," it replied sincerely.

Damn faeries—not only do you have to tell them the truth, they always seem able to tell the truth without saying anything, Wilson grumbled to himself. "Okay," he finally spat out. "Where and when?"

The little fae clapped its hands together at Wilson's concession, and strained its wings to be eye-to-eye. "Tomorrow at the thirteen hour then, druid, under the bells of the worship place. We'll be waiting for you," it spoke before popping out of existence.

Wilson exhaled. "It's over—it's safe to talk now," he informed her as he rolled off his knees. "Do you have a towel I could use to clean myself off with?"

Clark moved in stunned silence, rummaging through one of the many drawers in the shed. By the time she'd found an old kitchen towel, she'd also found her words, "That was simply amazing. What's the Magh Meall?"

"The land between this realm and the realm of the fae," Wilson explained, angrily daubing the paste off his chest. "It's sort of a buffer zone that both fae and humans can go to if they need to interact."

"All of it's really real, isn't it?" she marveled. "All the faerie tales passed down—"

"There is a grain of truth in many of the faerie tales," Wilson qualified as he dressed. "And most of them actually take place in Magh Meall, because if a human were to enter the actual land of the fae, they couldn't escape without the help of one of the grand faerie—who are generally not the helpful type."

Wilson looked over at Clark, who still had proverbial faerie dust in her eyes. "They look enchanting and sound beautiful, but they are dangerous. It's best to avoid them at all costs," he cautioned. Clark nodded in agreement; she was touched by his warning, which she mistook for concern. Wilson took the rag and wiped away all trace of the chalk—he didn't want to give Clark any ideas.

Wilson rose and extended his hand. "Thank you for letting me use your shed. Now, if you'll excuse me, I have to make a call."

Chapter Seventeen

Baltimore, Maryland, USA
1st of July, 8:10 a.m. (GMT-4)

Alicia Moncrief, codename Clover, was still in bed when she got the call. There was only number that bypassed her mobile's "Do Not Disturb" mode: Leader. As always, the instructions were brief and to the point: ASAP, London, Fulcrum, assault and murder by unknown fae—old and powerful, meeting in Magh Meall already arranged. She sat up and replied succinctly, "I understand. I'll be there within twelve hours."

Alicia Elspeth Hovdenak Moncrief was unlike the other Salt Mine agents in almost every way. First, she was young. At twenty-eight, she already had six years of experience under her belt. Second, there were no covers or aliases for Moncrief; she was recognizable to the greater world as herself—an independently wealthy heiress twice over. Since age eighteen, when her parents died in a plane crash over the Congo, she'd possessed the ability to do anything and go anywhere. Not only did she inherit the vast Moncrief real estate fortune from her deceased Scottish father, she also inherited the Hovdenak shipping fortune from her deceased Norwegian mother. And third, there was no need to convince Moncrief that magic existed. Her dear father and mother had left her with more than just land and wealth—

they'd left her with a solid knowledge of the supernatural and practice of the arts, as well as a vast repository of books and artifacts. It was a family tradition; both of her parents had been magicians as had their parents before them, and their parents before them, and so forth.

Moncrief was adrift after her parents' death. Once the grief had passed, she reveled in the freedom her wealth provided but after a few years of wandering, she found it an empty life. When you can literally do anything, the question of purpose and satisfaction became all the more acute and irrepressible. When a salt-and-pepper-haired woman of iron will tried to enlist her services, she initially turned her down. But Leader was persistent and persuasive, and after another year of listlessness, the then twenty-two-year-old Moncrief relented and accepted the offer, becoming the first Salt Mine agent from one of the old families. Leader had ordered her to keep her affiliation covert, as much of her usefulness to the Salt Mine relied on no one knowing she was an agent. Clover hid in plain sight, hiding her official duties behind the mask of a vivacious socialite, both in magical and mundane circles. Moncrief had just finished a long mission in the Middle East, where her connections granted her access to many of the ruling families and their entourages, and everyone always underestimated the petite busty bubbly blonde that was a hundred and thirty pounds soaking wet.

As Leader ended the call, Moncrief felt the rush of a new assignment wash over her. She extricated herself from bed and exited her expansive fourth-floor suite. "Gerard! Gerard!" she called out into the vast emptiness of her Mount Vernon Place residence. She stepped out onto the landing, ensuring her voice traveled down the wide wooden stairs that circled the walls of the mansion's expansive three-story foyer.

"Miss?" The dignified voice at the bottom of the stairs was unflappable.

"Ah, there you are," she remarked, peering down the railing. "I need to be in London immediately. See that the plane is ready in an hour, and pack my luggage."

"How many days will Miss be staying?" he inquired.

"I don't know. Probably less than a week? Let's pack for a five-day stay," Moncrief erred on the side of caution—in her experience, there was no such thing as having too much clothing.

"Consider it done," her long-time butler stated as fact. "Does Miss require anything else?"

"No, that'll be all. I'll be in the basement gathering additional material."

"Yes, Miss," the suited man affirmed, gliding into the back of the house and out of view.

Moncrief bounced down the ornate staircase, pausing midway to tighten the drawstring on her pajama bottoms to stop them from slipping down her hips. She followed the path of her servant to the back of the house and passed Gerard, who was making the necessary phone calls to ready her G650 before she descended the stairs into the basement. These stairs were purely functional and gleamed with generations of use from hard-soled, highly polished shoes. Her pace slowed as she cautiously descended them in her woolen socks.

She wended through the maze of shelves storing all manner of mundane supplies before she stopped at an old iron door inlaid with silver and gold sigils. She pricked her forefinger on the sharp tip of a nearby Javanese kris and traced a pattern upon the door using the blood. The crimson smear vanished into the cold smooth surface, and when she removed her hand, the door clicked open. She passed into the chamber beyond, closing the warded door behind her.

Although Moncrief had been entering the family vault ever since she was six, it still gave her a thrill. It was a two-story basement formed from granite fitted so tightly it didn't require mortar. It was internally waterproofed with several layers of Cocciopesto plaster, rendering the walls a dark brick red. Living sigils—mastered spirits of the dead forced into the enchanted walls—danced upon the plastered walls in a never-ending and ever-changing pattern that isolated the room from magical penetration.

The first rooms in the vault were dedicated to textile storage, and Moncrief pulled four outfits off their hangers—two sized for herself and two sized for Wilson. The fae were particular about unenchanted metal, and modern clothing was littered with them—buttons, buckles, zippers, and all the metal in bags, purses, and accessories. The outfits she chose were designed to be non-offensive to the fae; they were in earth tones and made entirely of linen with leather or wooden fasteners. Nary a hint of synthetic polymers graced the fabric, as that could be interpreted as a slight and the fae were not known to be easy going when offended.

With wardrobe selected, she rested the clothes on a long table and descended to the lower level. She passed the rows of bookshelves heavy with books and the magically protected cabinets holding items requiring isolation, and entered the family armory. The size of a spacious walk-in closet, the armory was a small room but filled with enchanted missile and melee weapons collected over many generations.

Moncrief didn't need to think about which weapon she would be taking and immediately plucked Carnwennan from its spot on the wall. It had been her father's dagger, and when it went down with him in the Congo, it had returned to her, appearing the next morning driven into the breakfast table. It had chosen him and then her, so she would choose no other before it—the famed dagger of Arthur himself was not to be denied.

Finding a weapon for Wilson was harder. He was a closed man, focused and unrelenting; selecting a weapon that would work with his personality wasn't easy. Each weapon in her arsenal had a temperament and history to consider. After half an hour of picking up a weapon only to put it back before moving on to another, she finally settled on Vlfberht. It was an eleventh-century sword with an unknown history, but it was one that never surrendered.

She carried both blades to the upstairs table, setting them

down upon the clothing she'd selected. Her final stop was the sealed cabinets. The first thing she grabbed was a pair of rings, named the Heart Rings, that rested in a plain cedar case. They were simple silver rings featuring a magnetite stone carved in the shape of a shield. She would wear one and Wilson the other, and the rings would pull any attacks aimed at one wearing the ring toward the other ring, potentially drawing metal weapons off target.

The second was a two-inch-long canine tooth hanging from a leather strap designed to be wrapped around the wrist. Called the Hound's Tooth, the yellowed tooth came from one of the hounds of the Wild Hunt, and it could track the undead, elves, or any of the fae. She slipped it into the cedar case with the rings and returned to the upstairs table, where she wrapped the weapons in the clothing, leaving one shirt out that she used to wrap the cedar case. Tucking the packages under her arm, she carefully made her way up the slippery basement stairs. Jules, her chef, was putting the finishing touches on her breakfast so she put everything down on the breakfast table while he served her.

"Gerard has informed me that Miss is planning a five-day trip?" he asked after she'd finished.

"Probably five, perhaps more," she answered flippantly. "If you'd like the days off, feel free, just make sure you don't go too far away."

"Certainly Miss, and thank you" he responded, carrying away her dishes.

She was halfway up the stairs when Gerard came out of her room, "The plane is ready for a flight to London, leaving in an hour and a half." His eyes briefly dipped to the bundle in her hands. "I've packed for five days and left two additional pieces of luggage for Miss for her various necessities. Do you require anything of me before you leave?"

Moncrief shook her blonde head. "I believe I have everything I need."

Chapter Eighteen

Luton, Bedfordshire, UK
1st of July, 11:05 p.m. (GMT+1)

Wilson waited in his new rental car next to the private northern hangers at the London Luton airport. He had traded in his Vauxhall for a Range Rover Velar once he knew Moncrief was en route—the little blue car wouldn't hold the masses of luggage she'd bring. Unsure how security would work, he'd arrived half an hour early, but it turned out to be no more than an ID check. He had bided his time watching the jets take off and land, rolling up the windows whenever the rain came in.

Wilson fired up the engine when he caught sight of Moncrief's distinctive G650 taxing its way through the drizzle to its final resting place and pulled alongside it when it finally stopped. Once the hatch on the plane opened, he exited the Range Rover and opened his wide umbrella to greet his backup.

Moncrief was the picture of style—a Fendi Zucca patterned trench coat wrapped around her petite frame and a matching bag in her hand. She gracefully descended the stairs that had dropped from the plane's door, and Wilson mentally gave her credit for wearing sensible shoes. "Damon! How nice to see you again," Moncrief bubbled as she neared the tarmac. Officially,

Alicia Moncrief was on the board of directors of the Institute of Tradition and, on occasion, deemed field visits necessary to ensure the organization was on the right course.

"And you as well, Alicia," he responded as she gave him a perfunctory hug complete with air kisses on each cheek. "Let me help you with your luggage."

Her effluent laughter erupted at his suggestion as the crew came down the steps bearing her luggage. "I forgot how funny you are," she remarked. "Be a lamb and open the back for them?" She had worked with Wilson enough to guess that he'd locked the car the second he got out.

He pulled the fob out of his pocket and a few beeps later, the crew carefully placed everything in the trunk. Wilson closed the hatchback and waited in the driver's seat while Moncrief gave last-minute instructions to the crew. *She really has "heiress socialite" down pat*, Wilson thought to himself as he watched the silent pantomime from within. The steely glint in her eye was present, but camouflaged with etiquette and smiles. Once she was aboard, he left the airport and hit the M1 going south.

"So, we're going into the Magh Meall?" she inquired in a serious tone that was at least half an octave lower than the one she'd used greeting him.

"Noon tomorrow, yes," he affirmed. "Did you bring everything we'll need?"

"Of course," she replied with an eye roll. "Where am I staying?"

"The Great Missenden Abbey. I booked you the bridal suite; it was the only room they had available on short notice," he explained.

"Mother always fancied me a summer bride," she smirked. "Where are you staying?"

"I'm at the Greysides, a few blocks north of you. I figure we'll meet in your room around ten o'clock tomorrow to prepare."

"Sounds good to me," she agreed. The wipers made another pass across the windshield. "Now, give me the complete story and what you think we're facing."

****

When Wilson returned to his room at the Greysides, his blue shirt was conspicuous lying on the ground near the corner of the dresser. He left the "Do Not Disturb" sign hanging on the door handle and readied for the séance. Once the small circle of tea lights was lit, he turned off the electric lights and sat down on one side, summoning his will as a whirling vortex. He was just about to start the customary supplications when a ghostly figure of a slim woman appeared opposite the glimmering circle.

"Mr. Warwick," Clara Felton addressed him directly, eschewing the conventional introductions and greetings of the séance. "Ever since you informed us of the attacks, we've been searching and have found the thing that's behind them!"

"I take it it's not a ghost?" he wagered a guess.

Her translucent eyes widened, "How did you know!"

Wilson sighed. Between the footage, Chloe and Dot's message, and the strange encounter with the rat rider, the probability of this being a ghost had rapidly diminished. "New developments have arisen since I first spoke with all of you, but your assertions have confirmed my suspicions." He hated eating crow as much as the next person, but a little diplomacy couldn't hurt if any ties had been unduly strained. "I fear I jumped to conclusions and should have been more patient before contacting you," Wilson replied contritely.

Miss Felton was unaccustomed to such consideration and graciously accepted his apology. "Do not feel too badly for your assumptions, Mr. Warwick. The creature has been disguising itself as one of us, but no ghost would wear a vest of human skin."

Wilson blinked twice. "Pardon?"

"You heard me right, Mr. Warwick, a vest of human skin!" she retorted and shivered a little. "Mrs. Wood was taking a walk through the park last night and saw it plain as day, just before it jumped into the massive ash tree."

"In the mortal realm?" he quizzed her.

"No, it walked the land of the dead," she answered emphatically.

"Did Mrs. Wood get a good look at the creature? Could

you describe it to me?"

Fearing that her words wouldn't be taken as the truth, Felton hesitated but eventually spoke, "She said it was taller than she, with beautiful green skin and eyes like emeralds. It carried a spear as yellow as gold. She…she said it bore the remnants of wings colored like a common blue butterfly, but they were severely clipped."

Wilson's stomach sank. *A faerie in the land of the dead?!*

"When did Mrs. Wood see this creature?"

"She found me immediately and I came to you right away," Felton reported. Wilson checked the time— his shirt was still on the dresser when he left to pick up Moncrief, so it couldn't have been more than two hours ago.

"And no one saw the creature leave the tree?"

The spectral young woman shook her head in the negative. "Sir John and Sir Hugh have been watching the tree since Mrs. Wood caught sight of it." She stared at Wilson for a while, watching him intently as he processed the information. "What does that mean, Mr. Warwick?"

"I'm not sure yet," he admitted, "but I'll do what I can until I know more. In the meantime, please let me know if this creature is spotted again."

Felton vacillated and finally screwed up her courage. "Are we in danger?" Mr. Warwick was known as an honorable and honest man among the spirit community of Great Missenden, but there were times when people would rather not know the truth of the matter.

"I don't know, but as a precaution, it wouldn't be a bad idea to tell everyone that isn't on sentry duty to avoid the park for a few days—three or four at most," he advised. Wilson knew the futility of telling either of the lords to stay away from the park; if they were going to be in the area, better that they should be helping him. They were still people after all, even if dead; they fared better when given a task. "I've put the blue shirt back on the dresser, if you need to contact me before then."

The ethereal figure curtseyed and faded from sight.

****

"That'll be twenty-four pounds, sixty," the tired-eyed cashier reiterated the numbers on his screen.

Wilson handed over a twenty and a five. "Here's a Smith and Churchill," he said, taking a stab at colloquialism.

"What?" the befuddled clerk inquired.

"Smith and Churchill and—they're the ones on the bills."

"Ah, yes," the clerk placated his lone customer; of course the guy buying a hundred pounds of salt at one in the morning was a nutter.

Wilson pushed the laden cart into the car park and loaded the bags of salt into the back of the Range Rover. Going shopping in the middle of the night was hardly his idea of a good time, but needs must. After returning the cart, he headed back to the suburbs of London.

The streets grew darker the farther he got away from the city and as he neared Abbey Park, he had his pick of the limited parking, choosing a spot as close as possible to the giant old ash tree. He slung the first bag of salt over his shoulder and trudged into the park. Once he unloaded all hundred pounds, he tore open one corner of the first bag and poured the white granules around the trunk of the old ash. Operating with the expectation of no rain in England was a fool's errand, but the drizzle earlier in the evening was light and the ground under the massive tree's canopy was relatively dry.

Wilson didn't know what type of faerie it was nor the kind of magic it was doing, but he knew a simple ring of salt around the tree would make it harder for it to operate supernaturally. It might not be enough to stop it, but hopefully, it would at least throw a wrench into its affairs. If nothing else, the salt would be visible—if only just—from the Magh Meall, and that would let him and Moncrief know where the ash tree's energy transferred over into that realm. He walked around the tree and inspected the circle before casting a charm breaker upon the salt. If there really was a faerie trapped within the tree, as he hoped, it would surely try to charm another creature to erase the circle. A charm breaker would break that charm once the charmed creature touched the salt. It was an old summoners' trick, and one that wouldn't stand for very long, but if he came back and found the charm breaker weakened but the salt circle still there, he'd know that he'd caught something. In that circumstance, he could repower the circle if needed.

With his work finished, he headed back to his tower room at the Greysides, allowing himself to enjoy the small high the charm breaker had created. He opened the door to find his blue shirt still on the dresser, and, before heading to bed, he checked his phone in the vain hope that Chloe and Dot had replied to his message about an unknown faerie wearing a vest of human skin that could somehow enter the land of the dead. They had not, but it had only been two hours since he sent the information.

He had unwavering faith in the twins' abilities to puzzle it out if given enough time, but time was of the essence. He and Moncrief had a date with the fae, and he didn't like the idea of going to the Magh Meall and relying upon the fae to provide him all the information he needed.

Chapter Nineteen

Great Missenden, Buckinghamshire, UK
2nd of July, 9:55 a.m. (GMT+1)

Alicia Moncrief poured herself another cup of coffee and slathered a bit of strawberry jam on the last bite of toast. The bridal suite was quite spacious, with room enough to comfortably maneuver despite her luggage. She breakfasted in the nook with views overlooking the park, while the four-post king-sized bed took center stage on the other end of the room. She half-heartedly made the bed and had just finished laying out the last of the gear, expecting Wilson's knock at any minute. She had never known him to be late, except for that one time, but he could hardly be blamed for being ambushed by a karakura. He was compulsively on time. Until then, there was always coffee.

Even though she had been up for hours, she'd elected to stay in her silk pajamas, collecting herself for the task ahead. Going into the Magh Meall wasn't difficult per se, but the fae could be trying on the best of days. She went over Wilson's conversation with the rat rider, looking for hints of what was to come, and it wasn't encouraging.

A crisp knock fell on her door at 10:00 a.m. sharp, and

Moncrief rose to greet her company. "Good morning, Damon. Right on time," she stepped aside to let Wilson pass through her door.

"Good morning, Alicia," he reciprocated and spied the controlled tempest that had whipped through the room: the remains of breakfast, the cluster of luggage, and their contents in various states of disorder. If he had to wager a guess, she was looking for something in particular and couldn't recall which suitcase she had put it in. Little did Wilson know that it wasn't Moncrief's fault—she had people to do the mundane packing; how was she to know where they put things?

"Coffee?" she offered as she neared the nook to finish her cup.

"No, thank you. I've already had two cups," he replied politely and his eyes ventured to the bed. Two beige linen suits were laid out over the duvet. Atop his clothing was an arming sword in a plain leather scabbard. Atop Moncrief's was a long dagger in a red-leather scabbard bejeweled with several different types of cabochon gems. Its hilt was wrapped in white leather that looked brand new, showing no stains of use. A ring rested next to each weapon and a strap of leather piercing a tooth rested near Moncrief's dagger. "Is this the kit you brought?"

Always down to business, she commented to herself. Moncrief hid her smirk behind her coffee cup and regained her composure by the time she had finished her coffee. "Yes, hopefully everything we need for a safe trip into the Magh

Meall," she answered, and bade him approach the bed. "We have your standard natural-fibered outfit sans metal."

"Naturally," Wilson affirmed as he hovered over his set of gear. "What about the weapons?"

Moncrief picked up the sword and placed it in his hands. "You will be carrying Vlfberht, an eleventh-century sword, probably of Viking manufacture. We're not entirely sure. Unknown provenance aside, it is an excellent weapon. It cannot be broken, it can injure all creatures, and when bearing it, you cannot be disarmed."

Wilson drew it from its scabbard. It was lighter than he'd expected, but arming swords always were. He checked the flat of the blade against his arm, moving it back and forth and inspecting the edge—*sharp*. He recognized the sigils embossed along the length of the metal. "So what's with the anti-summoning wards?"

"Ah, well, technically there are at least a hundred Vlfberhts," Moncrief explained, "and unless you guard the one you own against summonings, it can be called upon to replace another Vlfberht at any moment."

"Pardon?"

"That's how you cannot be disarmed—if someone knocks Vlfberht out of your hands, that weapon disappears and a new Vlfberht appears in its place. But don't worry, all the Vlfberhts are similar in power." She waved her hand dismissively.

"So if I get disarmed with this warded Vlfberht, does that

mean I walk away with two Vlfberhts?" Wilson conjectured.

Moncrief gave him a hard glare. "Don't be greedy, Wilson."

Even though she was three inches shorter than him and thirty pounds lighter, he felt chastised nonetheless. Wilson dropped the line of inquiry and backed up, giving Vlfberht a few testing swings and learning its balance. He was, as his sword master termed, *proficient* with the weapon, but he would rather use a firearm any day.

"And what are you carrying?" he queried. Moncrief had all the good old magical gear.

She picked up the dagger. "I'll be welding Carnwennan."

Wilson paused in mid-swing. "The Carnwennan?!"

"It was my father's. It chose me after he died," she replied nonchalantly.

"What does it do?" He knew the legends, but reality was inevitably different.

She pulled it out of the scabbard, moving it back and forth before him. "It's incredibly sharp, unbreakable, can damage anything my family's ever had the need to fight. And it can do this." Wilson watched as she slowly became less substantial, nigh translucent to the point that she nearly faded into the background.

"And the shadows wrapped Arthur and kept him from harm," Wilson quoted one of the old stories.

"Precisely," she responded, suddenly popping back into full existence.

"I'm assuming you've tested it in the Magh Meall?"

She placed the dagger back in its scabbard and didn't bother hiding her eye roll. "Of course. It works even better there. Bending the light, the fae call it." She knew he couldn't help himself from asking, but it was still insulting to question if she knew how her own weapon worked. "I've also brought some defense," she continued, turning his attention away from the weapons. "These are a set of Heart Rings; they draw attacks made by metal weapons toward the other.

"Nice," Wilson commented, sheathing Vlfberht and placing it back on the bed. "I've heard of them. There's only what, six pairs left?"

"Seven," she answered authoritatively. Wilson bowed his head at her greater knowledge. She picked up one and handed the other to Wilson. Even though they appeared to be the same size, it fit perfectly as they slid them on their respective fingers—nothing ever fit as well as a self-sizing magic ring.

"And finally, the Hound's Tooth, which I suspect will be the most important of our equipage. I'll keep that on me," she declared emphatically. "I've also secured provisions, if you've found a suitable location."

Wilson nodded affirmatively.

"Excellent!" Moncrief exclaimed. "Then, let's get changed. We have an engagement that can't be delayed."

****

Wilson had spent the early morning before meeting Moncrief scouting out an appropriate site for the ritual to enter Magh Meall, and he had settled on a forested section east of Abbey Park across the A413. It was about a quarter mile south of the parish church—remote enough that no one should disturb them, but close enough to hear the church bells. There wasn't parking nearby, so they left as soon as the hotel kitchen had prepared their picnic lunch. Their non-contemporary choice in clothing attracted less attention than Wilson expected from the staff of the abbey; they were intimately familiar with the strange vagaries of the wealthy, and there was little doubt that Ms. Moncrief was of such a class, even if she was clearly American.

Moncrief had brought a ridiculously large wicker picnic basket with her, large enough to stash their weapons and ritual equipment underneath the traditional checkerboard blanket and comestibles. Not that she had any intention of carrying the fully loaded basket—Wilson had to change arms several times during the walk from the car to the site.

When they finally arrived, Moncrief grunted her approval at his choice. Wilson placed the basket down and retrieved his folding trenching tool, encircling an area large enough for both of them to sit within. Meanwhile, Moncrief set up their picnic, which wasn't just a cover; entering the Magh Meall when hungry was a bad idea, and they would need to eat before performing the ritual.

The trough only had to be a few inches deep, so it didn't take Wilson long; by the time he'd finished, Moncrief was putting the final touches on the interior of the circle—the blanket was down, the food upon their plates, the candles at the cardinal directions, and a loose line of crumbled shortbread lined the interior of their circle.

After rearming themselves, they sat to a feast composed of egg and cress sandwiches, Scotch eggs, a Quiche Lorraine, and—Moncrief being Moncrief—a small tin of beluga caviar dished onto water crackers with a tiny bone spoon. Drinks were two bottles of water and two mini-bottles of Dom Pérignon to be consumed with the caviar. Hunger and thirst sated, they put the remains of the lunch back into the basket that was then placed outside of the circle.

They started the ritual five minutes before noon—a simple chant of supplication to the fae until the church bell struck noon. Only when the twelfth bell rang did their song end, and they closed their eyes for an hour of silent meditation. They encased the ring in their mind's eye by focusing their will, wrapping it around the entrenched circle like a winding a ball of twine. When the church's bells sounded the next hour, there were thirteen chimes, and they opened their eyes onto the Magh Meall.

As always, the first thing Wilson noticed was the smell. The middle lands smelled forever crisp and pure, like the first rush of spring, but it was more than that. It was like discovering a new taste or seeing a new color for the first time. Wilson conjectured that humans had sensory receptors that lay dormant in the mortal realms and were only triggered when they crossed into the Magh Meall—like the first time you tasted umami, but amplified throughout all your senses. The middle lands were a beautiful, sensuous overload, and it was easy for the uninitiated to get overwhelmed or intoxicated.

"Mmmm…" Moncrief hummed as the Magh Meall filled her senses. "So nice to be back." Wilson stood, offering a hand to his still-sitting companion. She accepted and dusted her seat off. "To the church?"

"That's where they said they'd be. I'd have liked to have been closer, but…" He shrugged. She nodded; there was no way they would have been uninterrupted for an hour of silent meditation in the middle of Abbey Park.

With their weapons at their waists, they left the safety of their circle. The lightly wooded area where they'd picnicked was now an old-growth forest with trees towering above them. Their vast canopy blocked out most of the purple-tinged sunlight, but there was plenty of light to determine their path from the angle of the sun. They made a beeline for their destination, looking for a break in the trees; holy places in the mortal realm created pockets of prairie amongst the massive trees found in the Magh Meall. Deserts did as well, but that wouldn't be germane to their situation.

They paused at the edge of the tree line abutting the church's prairie. There was no church, but the outline of the building stood translucent in the lavender light. Occupying the ghostly structure was a wilding of faeries—at least a hundred smaller faeries flittered around two human-sized fae. The female-presenting great fae wore a long shawl of azure-accented cloth of gold draped over a flowing diasprum shift, while the male-presenting one wore enchanted black chainmail with a tabard of azure-accented cloth of gold. Around both of their waists were the finest belts from which swords descended. They appeared human, but of a beauty that far surpassed what humanity was capable of producing. Their solid emerald green eyes were brilliant even from this distance.

"What are the fae of Tír na nÓg doing here?" Moncrief whispered, recognizing the telltale royal gold and blue. Tír na nÓg was an ancient land among the fae and home to the most powerful of their kind, the Tuatha Dé Danann. Those of Tír na nÓg did not often bother with the mortal realm, regarding it as a fleeting place that would soon be voided again and returned to its natural state in the next cycle.

Wilson shrugged, still taken aback at the power in front of him— only grand fae could take gendered form. Eventually, he whispered back, "I've never spoken with one before. You?"

She shook her head, keeping her eyes on the band. They stared a little longer before leaving the safety of their vantage point. As far as either of them knew, the Tuatha Dé Danann had never extended an invitation to a mortal—at least outside of legend—and neither wanted to keep them waiting.

Their exit created a stir among the smaller faeries, as dozens fluttered toward them in a kaleidoscopic cacophony of colorful butterfly wings.

"They are here! They are here!" Tiny voices pierced the calm of the Magh Meall. Soon, they were yelling between themselves.

"Beware! They are armed!"

"And ugly!"

"And enchanted!"

"So ugly! Their faces hurt us, do not look!"

Despite the heraldic cries of Moncrief's and Wilson's hideous visage, the two great fae remained impassive, their solid emerald eyes unblinking. Their only acknowledgement of the mortals' presence in the Magh Meall was their slow progress out of the center of the ghostly church toward the front doors.

The wave of prismatic wings hit Wilson and Moncrief, circling over them in a velvety torus. One of them landed on Wilson's shoulder; it looked like the rat rider he'd summoned, but he couldn't be sure. Telling individual fae of the same type apart was a difficult endeavor.

Wilson and Moncrief were about fifty yards away from the two great fae when the female raised her arms, silencing the little ones, who retreated behind their leaders. The rat rider left Wilson's shoulder and bumbled directly toward his mistress, landing on her outstretched hand. She quickly pulled off its wings before throwing it behind her, where it bounced several times on the ground before sliding to a standstill, unmoving. She passed one of the wings to her companion and they both consumed them, pressing the small iridescent morsels between sets of chitinous white teeth.

"Greetings," the female great fae finally spoke, indifferent to the fact that both Wilson and Moncrief had their hands on their weapons after her performance.

"I believe they are frightened," observed the male.

"We have not threatened them," she responded, perplexed.

"Mortals are strange creatures."

"We are strange creatures," Wilson responded neutrally, keeping his hand on Vlfberht, "who do not wish to be tossed away and consumed."

"Have no fear then," the female fae spoke. "You are distasteful. We will not consume you."

"Even if you make a promise that is far above your station and treat your betters as if they are your servants," the male responded, dismissing Wilson's ridiculous worry. "You are our guests for this visit and that requires consideration of differences in…" he struggled for the proper word.

"Culture," the female finished for him.

"Precisely. Culture," he assented with a small bow toward her.

"And for what purpose are we your guests?" Moncrief inquired, deliberately removing her hand from Carnwennan while nudging Wilson to follow suit with Vlfberht. He did not.

The two great fae looked at each other, whistling and clicking with remarkable speed. After a moment, they nodded to each other and the female spoke in a tongue intelligible to mortals, "We need you to kill one of our progenitors."

"Or capture," the male added, but both laughed loudly at the mere thought. *Mortals capture a Fomoir?*

Chapter Twenty

The Magh Meall
Summer Epoch

Wilson racked his brain, trying to recall what he'd read about great fae during the countless hours he spent in the Library stacks. Spurred on by their extended bout of lyrical derisive laughter, he plucked out a name from his memory. They were of Clan Dela—their emerald green eyes gave them away. He smiled, as if he was in on the joke, which only set everyone up for his cutting remarks. "I've always wanted to kill one of the Fomoire," he annunciated with precision. The tinkling laughter of the fae stopped cold, and Moncrief shot him a wide-eyed stare—she knew he was fully capable of being diplomatic, which meant he was deliberately being an ass.

"The creature brags," the female noted to the male.

"The creature believes he is *needed*," Wilson retorted, "and that he wouldn't be here if such a belief wasn't shared."

The two faeries visibly cringed at the word "needed." *Bingo*, thought Wilson. Faeries hated to be on the asking side of a bargain—to be on the weaker side was deemed beneath them, especially when dealing with mortals. They quickly regained their composure, and the male spoke, "You present as strong as we were led to believe."

"It certainly is confident," the female commented.

"Who exactly is your progenitor?" Moncrief asked in hopes of getting the conversation back on track.

"Morc mac Dela," the male answered. "He was captured and imprisoned a long time ago. I'm not sure how to say it?"

"Millennia, I believe that is their word for the long time," the female offered.

"So a thousand years?" Moncrief suggested, wanting to nail down a time for later investigation.

The two great fae guffawed again, and the feminine one corrected, "Oh, no! I have used your word wrongly. It was before you humans were here. Before this cycle, long before even we two were formed."

The fae waited to see if the revelation would elicit some response but were disappointed, confirming their suspicion that the problem with humans was that they had no sense of time or scope of importance. The female gave her counterpart a sideways glance and continued, "Morc mac Dela has escaped, and he is hiding in your world."

"And you want us to kill him. Or capture him," Wilson reiterated. "Which would you prefer?"

"Capture," they immediately responded in unison. The thought didn't seem as humorous as it had before.

"What did he do?" Moncrief inquired, curious as to what would make the fae imprison one of their own when they were renowned as masters of the artful curse that both punishes and controls.

The fae looked at each other and eventually the male responded, "He made a deal with an Earl of Hell and brought him to our realm—" Wilson coughed to hide his unsuccessfully repressed chuckle. The male fae waited for silence before continuing, "That had never occurred. The devils, the demons, they are forbidden from the fair realms. None have entered since."

"He found a way to break the forbidding, so he was locked away," the female summed up.

"So why wasn't he cursed?" Moncrief pressed politely.

The two great fae consulted again via whistling and clicking before reaching agreement. The female replied, "He was cursed. He…broke it. So we imprisoned him."

The Salt Mine agents kept their impassive miens despite their shock—neither knew of anything that *could* break a fae curse. The threat of a fae's bane was the main reason why promises to the fae were not taken lightly. "You caught him once, why not go after him yourselves?" Wilson quizzed them.

"*We* did not catch him," the female fae corrected the mortal. "Those before us caught him, and they are no longer with us. The way to the mortal realm is difficult for us and we would be greatly diminished there."

"But isn't Morc mac Dela diminished?" Moncrief posited.

"Yes, but he is a Fomoir, and the loss of his power in the

mortal realm would be considerably less than that of we true fae," the male spoke with some irritation at the fact that the mortals' questions, while reasonable, were highlighting their relative weakness in comparison to their ancestral progenitor.

"We could summon you to the mortal realm; then you'd retain your power," Wilson suggested.

"We are not common fae. To summon us would mean the creature would have to know our names, and our names are power," the female directly dismissed such a course of action.

Wilson was getting tired of being called "the creature" but buried his annoyance and focused on brass tacks. "If we decide to make a deal with you, what do we get in return?"

"When Morc mac Dela was interred, he had—"

"Interred, as in buried? Is he the living dead?" Wilson abruptly interrupted. He had never heard of undead fae, but it could explain why he was able to move through the mortal land of the dead.

"No, Morc mac Dela was interred alive in a tumulus tomb, which was his prison," the male clarified slowly; despite his limited experience with mortals, their obsession with death was known to him.

"So you just covered him with dirt and left him *buried alive* for hundreds of thousands of years," Moncrief explicitly unpacked their mode of punishment.

"Oh no," the female responded. "It was much longer than that."

"Yes, much longer," the male confirmed. "He was given three lightless stone-lined rooms within which to wander, and the stone chambers *were* covered with dirt. It's not far; we can show you if you'd like."

Wilson looked to Moncrief, who wasn't thrilled to be invited to a burial chamber that doubled as a prison, but could think of no better way for the Hound's Tooth to pick up Morc mac Dela's scent. She dipped her eyes and Wilson nodded before addressing the fae again. "Forgive my interruption, you were saying something about a possession of Morc mac Dela?"

"Ah, yes," the male fae found his train of thought. "He had a book in his possession when first interred, and he left it behind in his escape. It is no use to us, but to druids such as yourself, it should prove enticing."

"What's does this book contain?" Moncrief asked.

"Look for yourselves," the female suggested as she held up an empty hand. A sphere of rainbow light exploded in her palm, revealing a slim tome bound in hide—to Moncrief's keen eye, possibly alligator although it looked a bit off. The great fae offered the book to Moncrief, who kept her hands at her sides; she knew better than to accept anything from a faerie without explicitly determining the relationship of the offer. "Do you offer this to us without attachments, with the understanding that we will return it to you before we adjourn this meeting?" she asked.

The corners of the female fae's mouth twitched. "We do,"

she responded.

Moncrief was about to take the book when Wilson pushed her hand aside. "I would like to inspect it first," Wilson insisted.

"Certainly," Moncrief responded, trying to conceal her annoyance. "Be my guest." While Wilson considered his caution prudent, Moncrief felt it often crossed into redundant and tiresome.

Wilson gathered his will—*think, think, think*—straining against the walls of the middle lands. Here, he was significantly weaker than normal, perhaps not even half his normal strength, but performing magic in the Magh Meall had its benefits. First, there weren't any karmic costs; unlike the mortal realm, this place didn't punish practitioners for welding magic. Second, the euphoric rush that came with casting was notably absent, which allowed Wilson to use a wider array of spells without getting high, although he was sure there were some practitioners that would see that as a negative. He threaded his will around the book, caressing every ridge and turn, searching for magical hooks, curses, or traps. He found none.

"I don't see anything," he spoke to Moncrief, who accepted the book without comment. She held it vertically by the spine and let it fall open as it wished, an old trick to find the most-referenced section. When the pages finally settled, she quickly glanced at the contents and let out a short gasp.

Wilson was peeved that she'd revealed her interest to the fae, but his curiosity superseded. "What is it?" he asked, peering over her shoulder. She moved the book so both of them could see the genealogy graphed across the spread. He didn't recognize the family name across the top, but on the bottom right, circled twice, was the name Furfur.

"We'll do it," Wilson acquiesced immediately. "We accept your offer."

****

Once the terms of their agreement were hammered out, Moncrief reluctantly returned the tome to the great fae, who then led Wilson and Moncrief to Morc mac Dela's former prison. The stroll through the sunny Magh Meall amongst an entourage of faeries was enchantingly surreal, and true to their word, it was only a short walk to the southwest.

The mound itself was larger than Wilson had expected—over ten feet tall and a hundred feet in diameter. At the center of the mound stood a lone ash tree whose vast canopy spread high and wide. The two stone slabs that were once the doors of the prison were knocked aside, blasted open from the inside.

Wilson paused outside the tomb. "Have you been inside and cleared it out?" The fae verified it had been done, but he drew Vlfberht nonetheless. Moncrief followed his lead, holding Carnwennan in her right hand and Hound's Tooth in her left. Considering the unfathomable number of years he had spent here, the charm should have no problem getting Morc mac

Dela's scent.

Standing at the black entrance, the agents could feel the power running through the tomb even though its occupant was gone. They steeled themselves before entering. The creeping light of the Magh Meall went farther into the tomb than would normal light, but it wasn't very long until it was almost too dark to see. A quick whisper from Moncrief created a floating ball of light.

The walls of the tomb were uncut stone slabs that arched to a point in rough steps, and the floor was simple pounded earth. The orb of light illuminated the curtain of roots dangling from the roof of the small corbel-vaulted room. There were two corridors to the east and west that led to similar-sized rooms that were just as barren of possessions, but at least they weren't invaded by tree roots. Wilson figured that either the area had been looted thoroughly, or Morc mac Dela's prison sentence was mind-numbingly boring.

When they returned to the central chamber, Wilson pulled out his ivory saltcaster and blew a puff of salt into the heart of the chamber. It took only seconds to form into the same pattern he'd seen in the mortal world. His suspicions confirmed, he turned to Moncrief. "Has the tooth picked up the scent yet?"

"Let's find out," she replied, and released the tooth from her grip while keeping a firm hold on the leather strap wrapped around her wrist. The tooth shot out of her hand, pointing straight up toward the ceiling, straining at its leash. "I'd say we are good," she understated with a healthy dose of sarcasm.

"I wonder if that is the same tree as the one in Abbey Park—the one where the dead body was found," Wilson mused aloud. "I put salt around it last night, and if it is, our life got much easier."

"Only one way to find out," Moncrief replied as she sent her ball of light toward the exit. She extinguished it as they exited the tomb and the Hound's Tooth remained fixed on its target. The great fae were surprised to see such a thing in mortal possession, but held their tongues—clearly, they had chosen adequate mortals for the task. Wilson and Moncrief climbed up the short wall to the apex of the tomb and the massive tree. Wilson grinned as he saw a ghostly ring of salt around the ash and circled the entire tree just to be sure.

"Is everything satisfactory?" the female fae inquired when the agents returned from the top side of the mound.

"Yes, but I have two more questions," Wilson responded, pointing at the doors. "It looks like he just pushed his way out. Why did it happen now, after all those years of imprisonment?"

The two great fae whistled and clicked at each other. "When the prison was erected, it was powered by the grid of ley lines that lay beneath it," the male answered. "One of the lines has recently moved, weakening the fortification."

"Ley lines don't move," Moncrief scoffed incredulously.

"Of course they move," the female responded, and the tips of her fingers twitched; interacting with mortals could be so trying. "It's a matter of perspective that fleeting creatures may not appreciate. However, I will grant that this most recent shift is beyond typical variance."

"So one of the ley lines powering the prison shifted. Where did it go?" Wilson cut off the brewing tensions and steered toward more fruitful endeavors.

The female pointed to the west. "Not far. I could show you, if you wish."

"That would be appreciated," he responded with a small bow. As the two fae led the way, trailed by their butterfly-winged retinue, he shot a glance to Moncrief. She shot one back. They tacitly agreed not to argue until they left the Magh Meall, and Wilson wasn't looking forward to the incipient mincing of words. Technically, Moncrief was right, ley lines were not able to move permanently. But she was also wrong—ley lines could be bent, according to Chloe and Dot. Invoking the librarians was pretty much an argument-ender among Salt Mine agents, but Moncrief hated being wrong, especially about things supernatural, which she generally regarded as her birthright; any victory would be a hollow one.

They followed the fae another hundred yards, moving out of the field in which housed the mound and into the forest. When they stopped, the male threw up his arms and a glittering dust spread forth, coating a pulsating line that flowed invisibly along the ground.

"So this used to run through the middle of the prison?"

Wilson confirmed as Moncrief closely examined the ley line. She'd read about them, but had never seen one up close. In many ways, it was like a giant blood vessel; it had a beat to it—about thirty per minute—and smaller veins branched off of the main, quickly growing too thin to be seen despite the great fae's magic.

The fae nodded. "You said you had two questions?"

"Why did Morc mac Dela skin the torso of a human?" Wilson carefully phrased his question.

The cloud of butterfly-winged faeries erupted in a chaotic whirl at Wilson's question, and the female great fae had to yell twice to get them to calm down. "It appears that he has not given up on his schemes," the male remarked.

The fae exchanged looks and the female elaborated. "When you creatures arrived, we fae believed you would quickly pass, as all other creatures had passed. But when you showed a talent with the ways, some of us decided that you were a sign of the end of our cycle. Morc mac Dela is such a believer, and he swore that it was possible to conquer the mortal realms by finding a way to remain there undiminished in power."

"But wasn't he imprisoned long before we arrived?" Wilson puzzled. "He never even saw a human before he escaped, did he?"

"True, he had never seen one of you, but imprisoned does not mean he is ignorant or ignored. Some fae do not..." the female paused, pained by the words she must utter next.

"…Do not always obey our laws, and they spoke with him, seeking to gain power from his knowledge. In exchange for his wisdom, they taught him of your people, as well as other, more important matters."

"From what we understand," the male picked up the exposition, helping his companion shoulder the burden of sharing her race's weaknesses with mortals, "his plan to deal with you creatures is to make a suit out of your skins, a suit that would shield him from the unnatural emanations of your land, a suit that would allow him to remain there undiminished."

*****

Even though it felt like hours spent in the Magh Meall, Wilson's watch said it was 1:15 p.m. when they returned to the mortal realm. He immediately sent a message to the Salt Mine and tagged the request as ASAP SOS, so there was nothing to do but wait. The trek back to the car was a quiet affair once Chloe and Dot's names ended the argument about moving ley lines. They were both hungry, tired, and lost in their own thoughts. Wilson dropped Moncrief and her ridiculously large picnic basket off at the bridal suite at Great Missenden Abbey without even a halfhearted goodbye.

When he returned to his room at the Greysides, his blue shirt sat on the edge of the dresser. *No news is good news?* he thought hopefully, before descending to the pub. After a few beers and an ungodly amount of fish and chips, Wilson started to feel functional again. He pulled out his phone and searched his portable encyclopedia of the supernatural, hoping something would spark an idea of how he and Moncrief were supposed to capture or kill one of the Fomoire.

Wilson exited the pub as evening wore on, escaping the pre-commotion of the upcoming quiz night. He took a walk in the park and checked his ring of salt; it was still unbroken. It had been seven hours since he reached out to the Mine when his phone finally vibrated in his pocket. He unlocked the screen and frantically started scrolling through the message, pausing only to make sure Moncrief was cc'ed.

The beginning of an idea was starting to form, and Wilson mentally took stock of their resources to see if it was even possible. It was fussier than he liked—the more moving parts, the more points of possible failure. Wilson walked down High Street to Great Missenden Abbey and headed up to Moncrief's room.

She opened the door in her pajamas, phone still in hand and the remains of room service behind her. Wilson gave her a wolfish smile, which Moncrief would coin as "enthusiastically unfriendly." She knew that look and opened the door wide. God help her, Wilson had a plan.

Chapter Twenty-One

Morc mac Dela, in the shape of a red squirrel, huddled thirty feet above the ground inside the massive ash tree. Despite the summer showers, his fur remained dry. The rain barely penetrated through the leaves, and when an occasional drop did land on the lip of the hollow, it never splashed far within. All in all, it was a good nest, the kind of place he could hide and regain his strength, for Morc mac Dela was weak. Oh so weak.

He had spent eons entombed in his prison, so long that his feet had pounded the earth smooth until it was nearly as hard as rock. He had tried every method of escape—burn, burrow, fly, teleport—but none succeeded. Despite his constant attempts to break the wards with his will, they always held. All he could do was pace, read the book that had damned him, and practice with Gáe Buide, the yellow spear of Diarmuid Ua Duibhne, which caused injuries that would never heal. Even with the full might of the fae's forces mustered against him, they dared not separate the spear from its rightful owner.

He hadn't known how much time had passed alone in the darkness when the first of the fae approached the gates of his prison seeking his knowledge. They had been little more than voices on the other side of the warded stone slabs, but to Morc mac Dela, the connection to something beyond his three lightless chambers had become precious. He'd freely exchanged information for companionship; how his distant descendants had boasted of their prowess in stopping the great sheets of ice from washing away his prison, unaware of the power once wielded by the caged titan beneath the growing ash tree. Through these tête-à-têtes, he'd learned that the mortal realm was now filled with intelligent creatures that could think, speak, and wield power, despite their limited lifespan. Tales of their life force had reached his ears, how some refused to die after their mortal coil had failed them, and their essence carried on in another plane after their flesh returned to the dust from which it was made.

He'd spent much of his time thinking of these strange mortals, gathering as much information as he could from the faeries that dared to converse with him. He'd even spoken directly with one of these mortal creatures, one that had discovered his tomb and resisted his compulsion to break the stone slabs and free him. Oh, how the enchantments of the mound diminished his full will—he couldn't even charm a mortal through it! That creature had returned many times, trading knowledge for knowledge at each visit. It was from that mortal he'd discovered how to walk in the land of the dead, in exchange for how to place a mortal creature into a long and peaceful sleep that would only break under preordained circumstances.

The more he'd heard of the worlds outside of his tomb, the more ardent his desire to escape, but each time he'd tried, the wards held. Until one fateful day. It had only been through the countless failed attempts that he'd noticed the wards seemed weaker than before. Excitement stirring in his breast, he'd strained against them, but they held. Undeterred, he'd gathered his strength again and rushed headlong, but they endured.

Each attempt had drained him, and spent, he had had to rest, waiting until his full strength returned. In the dark quiet, where new hope roused desire long tamped down like the earth of his tomb, Morc mac Dela had decided he would rather extinguish himself than remain in his black hole. After his recuperation, he'd made his final bid for freedom with Gáe Buide in hand, channeling the entirety of his being through the yellow spear and pushing against the wards until at last they broke.

Staggering out of the tomb into the sweet air of the Magh Meall in summer, his elation had quickly soured—he was in greater danger than ever before. His escape had drained much of his power, essentially rendering him helpless before any great fae that encountered him. His unconquerable strength had been what forced them to imprison him; without it, they would have killed him all those eons ago.

With barely enough energy to remain corporeal, Morc mac Dela had shifted into a shape less costly to maintain while he still had the power to command Gáe Buide into his new form: a squirrel. Scuttling up the tree that sat upon his tomb and into a hollow, he'd put aside caution and entered the mortal realm, where he had been even weaker still but further out of reach of the fae.

His arrival into the mortal realm had not been the end of his immediate danger; the hollow he'd chosen had been occupied by an uncooperative gray squirrel and her three young. She'd refused to share her home and children with the newly arrived Fomoir, and the subsequent fight had nearly killed him. He'd triumphed in the end, eating the creature and its young for their needed sustenance, but his vitality had still teetered on the precipice. Between the drain of the mortal lands and the energy spent crossing over and in the fight, he had been so enervated that he could no longer master the spear contained within his changed form. Although it would remain with him, it would be no more than a simple spear in his hand until he regained enough power to force it to obey.

It had taken many small feedings over many days to stabilize his vitality to the smallest fraction of what it should have been. Thankfully, the mortal realm had been teaming with food. He'd gorged himself on simple animals and vegetative sources until he'd felt strong enough to overcome a larger creature—a feral cat he'd lured by taking the form of a rat. After a few such feasts, he'd felt confident to try his hand on one of the intelligent mortal creatures whose bright life force whetted his appetite and whose skin would shield him from the forces that decimated his power while he was so far from the true land of the fae.

His first attempt had been a disaster. In the dead of night, a group of mortals had wandered into his park, their life essence shining like a beacon to the power-starved Fomoir. Morc mac Dela had followed them in the shape of a bug, stalking them back to the abbey. For all he had been told about them, no words could have prepared him for how varied and ugly they were. He'd no idea there were so many different ways to be grotesque. He'd chosen the least hideous among them as his target, and waited until she'd separated herself from the pack and fallen asleep. Cloaking himself with bended light, he'd surrounded her, cutting and pounding against her meaty body to remove the skin he so badly needed. Unfortunately, he'd barely injured her before assistance arrived, forcing him to flee. The endeavor hadn't been a complete loss; at least he'd feasted on the blood he'd drawn from her before retreating.

In the face of defeat, he'd chosen to feed on lesser creatures to regain more of his strength before making a second attempt—at least enough to wield Gáe Buide once more. However, he'd been unable to resist another group of mortals traipsing by his park at night, this time with an elder who had knowledge of the land of the dead and those that called it home. Guided by the principle that fortune favored the bold, he'd followed them and had been rewarded when one of them separated from the pack and injured itself.

A direct attack had not worked in his favor during his first attempt at killing the intelligent mortals; consequently, he'd approached this quarry obliquely. Appearing as one of the sinister ghosts in their stories, he'd charmed the creature and cloaked both of them with bent light until they'd reached his tree in the park. There, he'd drained the wounded creature of its life force and blood. With his newfound strength, he'd taken its skin, forcing the edge of Gáe Buide against the sinew and fat until he'd liberated a vest to place over his true form.

Once the damp skin had encased his, he'd felt the palpable rush of power as the flesh suit curbed the drain of the mortal realm on his kind. The protection it gave had finally made him strong enough to master Gáe Buide again, and he'd rejoiced in his new vigor. However, he'd not anticipated the ruckus caused by finding one of their own dead—they had no such sentimentality among his kind. He'd resolved not to feed upon another one of them until he was certain his will could dominate large groups.

The next few days, he'd relentlessly hunted and consumed as much vitality as he could find throughout the park in preparation to cross into the land of the dead. It had been the perseverate thought that kept him company in the darkness ever since the mortal who'd visited him in his prison tomb instructed him on how to cross over. If he could enter that plane, he would forever be beyond the reach of the fae who hunted him—only the strongest fae could reach the mortal realm, and none of them could enter the mortal's land of the dead.

The ritual had been easy: collect life force without consuming it and instead place it within the skin vest, which would then carry him into the land of the dead. The transition had been unsettling to Morc mac Dela, a Fomoir whose senses were made for the land of the fae. The lackluster mortal realm had become even more washed out as the colors, smells, and sounds diminished among the realm of the mortal dead. He'd only wandered the vast grim emptiness for a few moments before he'd felt weaker, and a feeling of unease had settled over him as death pressed against him on all sides.

A hasty transformation back into red squirrel form, followed by a retreat into the mortal realm via his ash tree had been the only sensible course of action, but he'd rued it nonetheless. During his recuperation from the trip, he'd reconsidered his plan and found its flaw—if he wished to spend any significant time there, he would need a complete skin suit, not just a vest. Despite the trial and error, Morc mac Dela had been pleased overall with his progress up to that point, but while he'd pondered his necromantic suit, someone surreptitiously circled his tree with salt.

When he'd first found its restraint upon his movement, he'd tried charming a passing bird into disrupting the salt, but the stupid thing had ignored his command upon the first touch of the substance. While the salt had looked unremarkable upon examination, he suspected there was an enchantment upon it. After fuming for hours—*how dare mortals use power!*—he'd regretfully reached the conclusion that the mortals had developed magics to which he was not yet attuned, magics that were invisible to his Fomoirean senses.

Morc mac Dela grunted angrily into the night, trapped in his ash tree. With the same persistence he'd applied during his first imprisonment, he descended the mighty tree to once more test the circle of salt. He rounded the trunk a few feet off the ground, pressing against the circle with his meager will, but it held against the pressure. He froze, clinging to the side of the tree with his sharp claws as footsteps disrupted the pitter-patter of the soft rain.

Two creatures approached his tree, their incandescent life force heralding their approach from far away. Morc mac Dela scurried up the tree for safety and watched intently as they added more salt to the circle and cast another spell; a crimson snake threaded its way through the white grains before fading into nothing. They held their tongues, ensuring their silence robbed him of information, but the throbbing weapons at their side spoke for them.

The ancient Fomoir readied Gáe Buide for battle—they

would not be able to maintain the circle when a heavy rain came, and when it faded, he intended to drain them both of their vitality. Even in his lessened state, he did not doubt his power against two mortals now that he'd re-mastered his fearful yellow spear. But eons of imprisonment had also made Morc mac Dela cautious; the freedom recently earned had been taken away from him by the mortals, and he would not allow himself to be permanently trapped again. As a precaution, he loaded his fleshy vest with the life force of a slug—if all else failed, he would flee before them and gather his full strength elsewhere.

Chapter Twenty-Two

Moncrief finished her circumambulation around the park, ensuring they were alone. She stopped in the thick foliage that covered one of the least-used entrances into Abbey Park. "We're all clear," she verified to Wilson. "Are you ready?"

"Let's do this," he replied grimly, retrieving Vlfberht from under his jacket and belting it on. His Glock 26 rested in its shoulder holster, but if things went as planned, he wouldn't have to use it. In fact, his gun was a last resort—immediately banishing Morc mac Dela back to Tuatha Dé Danann could throw a massive wrench into everything he'd carefully crafted over the past two days.

They made a beeline for the ash tree, halting a few feet from the salt circle. Wilson filled his left hand with the iron shavings he'd previously enchanted and drew his blade with his right, thankful for the cloudy night sky that obscured the moonlight. The last thing he needed was to draw attention to his sword. He nodded at Moncrief, who had Carnwennan in hand. She edged forward and swiped a thin line through the salt with her toe.

The instant the circle broke, Morc mac Dela appeared in full radiant and fearsome form, but neither Wilson nor Moncrief had time to appreciate his terrible beauty as they zeroed in on two lightning-fast stabs of Gáe Buide. The golden yellow spear split in twain at the last second, attacking both agents simultaneously.

It would have ended there, but for the drawing power of the Heart Rings—each iron end pulled the strike toward the other, throwing Morc mac Dela's careful aim off balance. The slight miscalculation of the spear was all Wilson and Moncrief needed to block the attacks with their weapons, and in the moment's respite, Wilson threw his handful of iron shavings at the Fomoir, coating him with countless slivers of iron no bigger than caraway seeds.

Morc mac Dela roared in pain as the iron burned his skin. Enraged, he lashed out with Gáe Buide, but as the spear twisted in twain again, Moncrief called upon the power of her blade and blinked out of existence. *How can a mortal bend light as if she were fae?* Morc mac Dela fumed as his spear missed both targets once more.

From the shielded darkness, Moncrief gathered her will and whipped against the flesh coat worn by the Fomoir, slicing off a hand-sized piece and weakening its protective power. As the skin fell, Wilson pressed forward with Vlfberht in a left Pflug attack; even if Vlfberht didn't find purchase, at least it would force the Fomoir's spear up and over Wilson's shoulder, rendering Morc mac Dela vulnerable to a stab from Carnwennan.

As the Fomoir stepped backward to reduce the thrust's effectiveness, he stumbled on a rogue tree root that just broke the surface of the soil. Thrown off balance, he tried to bend light, only to find himself unable. Panicked, he attempted to shape change, but to no avail. In that split second, Morc mac Dela realized he was in actual danger. Not only did his opponents wield the power, they knew of him, his abilities, and how to stymie them. He couldn't shift or disappear from their vision as long as the iron shards searing his skin remained, so with the speed of a thought, the Fomoir fled into the land of the dead, hoping to put distance between himself and the two murderous mortals. He would quickly return to their realm, but well out of the reach of their senses and free of their traps.

In the mortal realm, the magnificent Fomoir with the delicate azure wings never reached the ground, blinking out of existence before he hit. Moncrief stabbed where he was last with Carnwennan, just in case the twins or Wilson were wrong about the iron shavings preventing him from going invisible. "He's gone," she called out as her dagger found empty air.

"Holy shit that bastard's fast," Wilson exclaimed, backing up and readying another handful of iron shavings. "And that spear...magnificent!"

****

Morc mac Dela fell face-first onto the ground in the land of the dead, and he immediately felt his power diminished by the increased distance from his home. As he pushed with his arms to rise, pain seared through his back and radiated down his body. Spinning over, he saw an armored figure looming over him wielding a sword and shield; the Fomoir's bright purple blood dripped off the end of the long, shimmering blade.

"Begone, foul creature!" the warrior cursed, swinging his weapon again. Morc mac Dela rolled left, barely avoiding the blade. Another blow rained down, and the elder fae took full advantage of his inhuman speed, quickly dodging the attack and gaining his feet for a counterattack with Gáe Buide. The golden spear bit deep into the ethereal figure, but to no effect. As he pulled the spear back for a second attack, he started to feel the life-sucking force of the land of the dead; recognizing his presence more readily the second time around, the realm sought to actively relieve him of the burden of life.

"Your weapons are useless here!" the warrior mocked him. "To me, Sir Hugh!" he cried out. Another similarly dressed and armed figure came around the trunk of the massive tree astride a champing destrier. Faced with two opponents and a weapon that couldn't injure them, Morc mac Dela turned his will against them, burning his life force to push them away. The two warriors were repelled, but the edges of his skin vest caught fire from the life-filled energy he wielded, forcing the Fomoir to tamp out the flames with his left hand.

"Your magics come with a price in the land of the dead, demon!" Sir John yelled as he charged the green-skinned and emerald-eyed obscenity, only to run through empty space as Morc mac Dela ran once more through the planes to the last place he wanted to see again, but to the only place free of immediate threat—the Magh Meall. Sir John laughed and cleaned the filth off his blade. "Just like old times, son," he hailed his fourth son, who was returning to his side of the tree they'd promised to guard for Mr. Warwick.

****

Morc mac Dela appeared atop the ancient mound that had been his prison for eons. The Magh Meall was much closer to his home plane, and the elder Fomoir felt a measure of his vitality return despite his wounds and the small bits of iron that burned his skin. He was far weaker than he preferred, standing this close to his former tomb, but he took solace in the fact that he was still alive and alone to regroup.

He dropped to his knees and leaned against his faithful golden spear, catching his breath after the quick succession of plane changes. The fragrant air was all the sweeter after his time among the mortals. He would never have guessed Gáe Buide would be ineffectual in the land of the dead, being an extension of death itself and deadly to all creatures he had ever encountered. *Perhaps death had no power in the land of the dead?*

Regardless, he had learned and he had survived, and there was little doubt in his mind that he would eventually conquer it. Unlike mortals, he had all the time in the world. He was there before them and he would be there after they had passed. Rested, he rose, placed Gáe Buide against the ash, and began picking off the annoying bits of iron burned onto his skin.

Suddenly, his spear flew away from the tree and into the hands of one of his children that emerged from thin air. As the spear touched her hand, a wave of energy rippled through the Magh Meall, revealing a quiet army surrounding his barrow.

And then the lightning started and Morc mac Dela knew no more.

Chapter Twenty-Three

Antipodes Island, New Zealand
11th of July, 2:00 p.m. (GMT+12)

The fifty-foot yacht *Angitu* sliced through the rough subarctic water a mile off Anchorage Bay, the only bay on Antipodes that was suitable for offloading its cargo. It had been three difficult days of travel from Dunedin, and the captain, Jack Anderson, smiled in relief once they were close enough to trim the sail and slowly glide into the relative safety of Hut Cove. He'd timed it perfectly: the tide was receding and his passengers would have a solid six hours to get in and out.

There were two of them—a man and a woman, but he wouldn't have called them a couple—with a package to deliver to the research team on the island. A curious and gregarious fellow, he'd tried to coax them into conversation during the long trip, but they'd been remarkably close-lipped. Normally, he would have pressed the issue, but they insisted that was all he needed to know and the exceptional pay swayed him to their thinking.

They were decked out in warm water-resistant clothing, waiting at the back of the boat near the inflatable launch. The cold gray sky starting spitting snow as the *Angitu* slowed to a stop, dropping both anchors. Other captains preferred a single anchor, but he preferred to keep his sails rigged—halyard on the main and minimum sail size—in case his engine refused to cooperate when it was time to leave; ergo, the double anchor. Once he and his crew of two secured the ship, he gave the all-clear signal to his guests and they launched the smaller vessel, turning the engine over when they were two boat-lengths away.

****

Wilson was glad to finally be back on land. He wasn't seasick per se, but tired of the endless waves of cold gray rolling water since they'd left Dunedin. It was a stark contrast to the long sunny summer days they left behind in England, although he didn't hate traveling by private jet. As they neared the beach, he and Moncrief pulled the inflatable boat onto the rocky landing and secured the craft: the anchor dropped with a second rope wrapped and tied to a nearby large rock.

He passed Moncrief her backpack and donned his own. They didn't know what they were going to encounter, but they knew it was enough to bend ley lines on the other side of the earth. Accordingly, they came heavily loaded to deal with all manner of possibilities.

Once the Mine knew of the displaced ley line without an apparent local cause, it didn't take the twins long to point the finger at an antipodal change. From there, it was a simple matter of geography to locate where Fulcrum and Clover needed to go next and whittle down their possible targets. There were only four people on the Antipodes: two married couples who were researchers from the New Zealand Department of Conservation, engaged in a long-term biodiversity study of the islands after the successful rat eradication efforts of the prior year. The Davidsons were in their late twenties and researching land-based biodiversity while the Wangs were in their early fifties and studying the island's shoreline, taking them away from the main camp for multi-day stints.

Wilson and Moncrief struggled up the rough terrain near the shore until they reached the main plateau of the island. There, they spotted the Castaway Hut along with a new secondary building in the far distance. Standing in front of the hut were two people—a man and a woman whom Wilson guessed were the Davidsons, but at this range, he couldn't be sure. Wilson and Moncrief made no effort to mask their approach—they didn't have that sort of time. The clock was ticking for their return boat back to the mainland.

The trudged their way through large tuffs of grass and mossy boulders until they reached the site of a recent landslide—the soil on the Antipodes was thin and peaty, and would slip over the hard rock beneath during heavy rain. By the time the two agents cleared it, the Davidsons had decided to come out and meet their new guests.

"Hallo!" the scientists yelled with big waves.

Wilson waved back, but the two agents opted to say nothing until they were within speaking range. "I'm dreadfully sorry about this," Wilson spoke as he and Moncrief pulled their firearms at their approach, "but we need to talk to you about something important and we don't have time to waste with niceties."

The Davidsons were stunned, but came to their senses and raised their arms. They were literally in the middle of nowhere and they were going to be robbed at gunpoint?

"Good. Let's go back to the hut and get out of this weather. You lead," Wilson ordered.

The researchers turned back and led the agents into the modest hut, most of which was given up to scientific instrumentation and record keeping; a table with tools, two chairs, and a small closet for storage. The other side of the room contained a foldout couch, a camp stove, and a dining table big enough for two. They ordered the Davidsons onto the couch and pulled the two chairs on the other side of the room to keep a safe distance between them.

"We don't have anything of value here," Rebecca Davidson blurted out once they took a seat. "We just have our research and some food. You can take both if you need them."

"We're not here for your research, Mrs. Davidson," Wilson responded. The fact that he knew their names visibly upset the couple. "We're here to determine if you know what you're doing, or if it's accidental."

Confusion washed over the couple's faces. "We're here to do a full biodiversity study?" Robert Davidson answered with hesitation. "After the rat—"

"We're not interested in the rats," Moncrief interrupted. "We want to know about the magic."

"Magic?!" his wife exclaimed.

"Yes, the magic that's happening on this island and causing problems in England," Wilson cut to the chase.

Dear Lord, they're bonkers and they have guns! thought Robert. He was a scientist at heart and his weapon of choice was reason and evidence, but there was little that could be done with crazy. He steeled himself; if only they'd sat closer, he'd have a better chance of rushing one of them.

Moncrief pointed to the wall above and behind the scientists. "There's a cross and there's a pentacle. In my experience, if someone's taking the time to hang a pentacle, someone's taking the time to work magic."

"Yes, we're Wiccans," Rebecca quickly agreed. "The Wangs are the Christians, but they're fine with us practicing our religion. We're not hurting anyone."

"And yet things have gone wrong," Wilson spoke in the contrary. "Which of the rituals have you been performing?"

Rebecca's brow furrowed under the stress. "Since we arrived, there was Samhain and then Yuletide, and of course our daily prayers. We haven't done anything new or unusual."

The agents looked at the two scientists—their fear was

apparent, as was Robert's as yet executed heroic thoughts. "I don't think they know anything," Wilson finally said to Moncrief.

"I agree. Something else is going on here. I'll salt and see what comes up."

Wilson grunted in approval, keeping his Glock 26 steady on the scientists as Moncrief dug her saltcaster out of her backpack. Wilson carefully watched the scientists' faces while Moncrief prepared—he wanted to judge their reaction if a pattern formed. The white grains billowed out from Moncrief's saltcaster in the space between them, and then rushed toward the back wall of the hut, forming a single line hanging off the closet door like a pencil thrust into the wood. The terrified looks on the Davidsons' faces confirmed that they knew nothing. Their reaction was so strong, Wilson hurriedly glanced behind him to see what had happened.

"Are you seeing this?" Moncrief quizzed Wilson's brief glimpse.

"What do you have in the closet?" Wilson focused on the couple—whatever was back there was active and powerful as hell.

The Davidsons exchanged looks of disbelief and confusion. "Just storage for the stay and…the mokomokai?"

"The what?" Moncrief inquired.

"Mokomokai," Wilson answered her before they could respond. "Mummified heads of important Maori peoples. The question is, why do you have one here? They belong to their tribes or to the Museum of New Zealand Te Papa Tongarewa, if unclaimed by a tribe."

"The Wangs found it washed up on the shores of South Bay, and they lugged it back here before opening it," Robert replied. "It was inside a sealed jug within a rotting wooden crate. We're planning to hand it over to the museum when our study's over."

"That's got to be it," Moncrief said to Wilson.

"When did it wash up, and did you touch it?" Wilson grilled the scientists.

"It'd be four months ago," Robert responded.

"Closter to five," his wife corrected him. "We're supposed to leave next week, remember?"

"Yeah, nearly five months then," he agreed.

"Did you *touch* it?" Wilson repeated.

"Well, yeah, we touched it—we took it out of the jug, but we didn't damage it," Robert answered defensively.

Moncrief looked at Wilson, who nodded. "These daily prayers," she addressed Rebecca. "What are they about?"

"Mostly I pray that the island recovers from the damage we've done to it and…" she paused momentarily and bit the inside of her cheek, a nervous tick when she got embarrassed. "And I've also started to pray over the adoption we've decided to start once we get back to the mainland."

Moncrief shrugged and threw up her hands. "That's got to

be it."

Wilson kept his weapon focused on the couple. "Yeah, prayers of restoration and healing, coupled with familial bindings? That's it. I'll get the head, you keep them where they are."

Moncrief nodded, trading her saltcaster for her gun while Wilson opened the closet door, disrupting the salt; the granules dropped to the floor, its magic spent and dissipated. Once the door was open, he could feel the item within, seething and grinding in the darkness of its earthen pot. Wilson was relieved the scientists had wrapped rope around the rotted crate—it was that much further removed he could stay from the palpable power within. Using both hands, he gingerly picked it up and suddenly realized that he'd been wasting his life doing what he'd been doing. What he really needed to do was open this crate.

Think, think, think. Wilson focused his will and pushed aside the compulsion. "It's self-aware and aggressive—bastard tried to charm me!" he yelled back to Moncrief as he maneuvered the crate outside the closet. "This is it, all right. When we get back to ship, we need to get as much salt around it as possible."

"And these two?" Moncrief asked.

"They didn't do anything wrong," he concluded as he closed the closet door with his foot.

"Do you think they can keep their mouths shut?" She kept a firm hand on her gun and looked the huddled couple directly in their eyes. Moncrief prided herself on her ability to summon her crazy eyes.

"I don't know," Wilson played along—he wasn't used to being the good cop. "Do you think you can keep your mouths shut?" Wilson asked them.

"Damn right we can," Robert responded as Rebecca vigorously nodded in agreement.

"Well then, our problem's solved. You are aware that we know who you are, what you do, where you live, and where your families live, right?" Wilson spoke deliberately slow.

"And that if you say anything, we'll make sure that nothing more gets said," Moncrief turned up the crazy.

"And that goes for the Wangs as well, because they'll surely ask what happened to the floating head they found," Wilson added.

The scientists nodded.

"We'll be on our way, then. Best of luck with the adoption."

Epilogue

Great Missenden, Buckinghamshire, UK
11th of August, 11:00 a.m. (GMT+1)

Joy Ejogo stared at the wall of oils and froze; she couldn't remember if she needed linseed oil or almond oil.

"It's okay to consult your notes when you first start out. You're not expected to have these things memorized on day one," Vivienne Clark advised Ejogo from the bench. "I've been doing this for almost forty years, and even I need a refresher on the rare rituals. Just remember, anything worth doing is worth doing right."

Ejogo bobbed her head and reviewed her ingredient list again and reached for the almond oil. When she'd first received the call from the Institute of Tradition, she thought it was scam and kept waiting for them to ask for her personal information. It had seemed too good to be true—make three thousand pounds a month working from home? Her suspicions retreated once she'd found out that Vivienne Clark had recommended her for the position and would train her.

Ejogo moved away from the racks of oils and toward the other jars of components, picking out what she needed for the weekly ritual. She had observed Clark last week, and this week was her turn. Everything was so tidy in Clark's shed, perfectly set up for her non-art work. It would take Ejogo time to set up her own space, especially with Aaron getting into everything, but Clark had offered her use of her shed until she could find a suitable place with the advance the Institute had given her.

Ejogo swept aside a rogue tuft peeking out from the scarf she used to tame her hair and approached the polished slab of slate and carefully measured out each of the constituents at the dais. She kissed her finger and touched it to her third eye three times and began the recitation. Clark watched her pour the almond oil and add each element to the offering in time with the litany. When Ejogo closed the ritual, Clark asked her how she felt.

"Good," she answered pensively. "Lighter."

Clark smiled. "I think you'll do well with the Institute. Now, we must log your performed ritual." She handed the younger woman a thick leather-bound book with thick pages that smelled faintly of vanilla. "It's time we started your journal."

THE END

The agents of The Salt Mine will return in *Mirror Mirror*

Printed in Great Britain
by Amazon

66479189R00125